OK Danny Boy

Part One

(CHAOS)

By

Felicia Johnson

Published by: SPE Media, Productions & Publishing, LLC
Editor: J. Cameron
Cover Design: Lacey O'Connor
Photography: Michael J. Feifer Photography

To learn more about Felicia Johnson and to watch the live action book trailers for "OK Danny Boy" please visit www.feliciajohnsonauthor.com.

For SPE Media, Productions & Publishing, LLC please visit www.spempp.com.

This book is dedicated to Barry, Marcus, Tyler, Frankie, Lorenzo, Anthony, Victor and Angelo.

INTRODUCTION

Dear friends,

Thank you so much for your continuous strength and bravery as we continue to fight against the stigma attached to mental health issues. While mental illness is more freely discussed these days, it is still hard to approach families, friends, and colleagues about these issues.

I wrote "HER" in dedication to my late best friend, Holly. Holly was my best friend when we were fifteen years old. She was the first person that I ever felt truly comfortable enough to open up to about my own mental health issues. We helped each other. Holly committed suicide nine months into our budding friendship. Although, Holly has passed on, she left me with a lifetime of friendship and inspiration that led me into the work that I am doing today. When I named my first novel "HER", it had nothing to do with the main character, Kristen Elliott. The book was for her, Holly. Therefore, I couldn't think of a better title. Dedicated to her, my best friend, forever.

"HER" was originally supposed to be three books. As you read "HER", you will see that it is a thick book! However, it is broken into three parts. I wanted three books as it was originally written. However, my publisher, at the time, was not up for that idea. She reasoned with me, "Why leave readers in suspense and wonder with a story that is highly emotional and filled with useful knowledge? Releasing it as one book could serve people better to help educate them about mental health issues." I saw her point, and I agreed.

"HER" is a big book with a story that is written in fiction for readers to get inside of the mind of someone who is struggling with mental illness. Readers get to see from a first person point of view what it is like to have a mental breakdown, go through treatment and eventually get into recovery. "HER" has a heart of a text book, to help educate, enlighten and move readers to learn more about themselves and their loved ones who may be suffering.

With "OK Danny Boy", my goal was to write a story that shows the point of view of a person who struggles with a physical illness as well as mental illness. I hope to help readers open their eyes to what the stigma looks like from the point of view of a young man who feeds the stigma himself. He eventually learns to fight against it with the support of friends and family. This kind of healing takes him on a long journey of difficulties with hard lessons to learn and adversities over which to triumph.

"OK Danny Boy" is a three book series. Yes, this series *is not* like "HER". Daniel is a different force. He is the voice of those who struggle with both physical and mental illness. Perhaps one day I will tell you about who inspired Daniel's character in "HER". That same person has inspired me to write Daniel's story and bring his voice out and onto paper.

This series starts out with a conversation that Daniel and Kristen are having with each other while they are both in Bent Creek Hospital. If you go back to "HER" and read Chapter 36, you will read the conversation from Kristen's point of view. Chapter one of "OK Danny Boy" begins with that same conversation. However, chapter one is from Daniel's POV. From there, Daniel tells the story of his life before Bent Creek. Daniel reaches deeply within himself, in order to give us an in depth look into his background and find out what lands him into Bent Creek Hospital.

Daniel's journey is much different from Kristen's story. Their voices are different. Each character has their own set of emotions, experiences and backgrounds.

I hope that you will enjoy this series. I do not plan to make you, the reader, wait too long between the releases of each book in the series. These stories are emotional and telling of each character that deals with their own sets of issues. It is important to keep educating others and ourselves in order to continue to fight, win the battle and end the stigma.

Best wishes,
Felicia Johnson

"For now, I'll stay inside of my head until the man with the needle says that I must go. And where I go from there, even I don't know." ~ Abysmal Vein

PART ONE

CHAOS

CHAPTER 1

"My father probably would have killed my mother. Theresa probably would have killed herself, and I probably would have done it, too," I say.

"Were you scared?" Kristen asks.

It is the first time anyone has ever asked me that question. I think about her question for a moment. I sit across the table from a girl who looks like she could break at any moment. I want to be careful because I have a feeling that if I say the wrong thing, look at her the wrong way, or even make an offensive noise, she will start crying. Although, at this very moment, I am holding in a serious gas bubble that wants to pop right out of my ass. I release it, silently. Relief. I don't care anymore.

Kristen is a peculiar girl. She doesn't seem to say much. Her emotional outbursts, dramatic facial expressions and bandaged wrists tell me a lot about her. She is broken, like most of us who are doing time in Bent Creek Hospital for various mental health issues. We are the lost and troubled teenagers with screwed up parents, a raw fetish for self-harming and sick regrets of our suicidal tendencies. It's kind of like a messed up joke to think about how many times we fail each time we try to die, but we don't really want to die. It feels like one more thing that we can't seem to get right.

Kristen has scars up and down her arms and a frown that sticks to her face. When we first met, Kristen's frown was the first feature I noticed. Janine introduced her to everyone on her first day. Kristen and Janine are roommates. We all have roommates. Unfortunately, even I had one. His name was Rocky. He is no longer here.

Patients at Bent Creek Hospital are separated into co-ed groups. The groups keep the numbers of jaded youth from growing too large against the smaller numbers of therapists and counselors who treat our mental health complexities. Their jobs are to shrink our minds from overwhelmed humans to zombified dust bunnies with state of the art coping mechanisms, new findings from studies of techniques that prove useful for young minds such as DBT and CBT along with the latest, shiny new drug. At least, that's what I used to think about the system.

Right now, I'm off most of the meds that my doctor had put me on. But I still have to take the daily medication that helps keep me alive.

I can't believe it. I can't believe most of the things that I've seemed to overcome in the last few weeks. It seems as if the events that took place before I came into Bent Creek Hospital happened years ago instead of weeks ago. That person who broke down and couldn't cope with what had happened doesn't seem like it was me. But it was. If it weren't for Dr. Finch, Dr. Bent, Dr. Pelchat and people in my group like Janine, Kristen, and Tai and unbelievably, even Rocky, I wouldn't have noticed the difference in myself.

We are all together in *Group One*. It must be fate because all of us seem to have the same diagnosis of sorts. Diagnoses range from some form of depression, whether it's Bi-Polar I or Bi-Polar II, mixed with something else; a dual diagnosis? I don't know. While the other groups have their dissociative identities, hair eaters, schizophrenics and the demonically colorful personalities of the insane youth with sociopathic and psychopathic tendencies, our group seems to dwell right in the middle of those who don't seem to fit just one single problem. We don't have a problem. We have *problems*. Plural. Therefore, I was given a couple of diagnoses of Bipolar I (complete with manic episodes and Major Depression) and Obsessive Compulsive Disorder also known as OCD. Having to deal with that on top of having Juvenile Diabetes seemed to be enough to keep the medicine cabinet full at home.

Looking at Kristen is a lot different from when I look at Janine. Janine is obviously thin. She could be mistaken for a model except she has some major flaws that probably would keep her off a runway. She isn't naturally thin. I can tell that she makes herself that way, unhealthily. Dark purple pools circle the skin around her eyes like bruises. Janine tries to wear make up, but she has to put on so much of it to cover up her discolored skin. Her hair is long, but it is thinning. Her teeth and fingers are discolored from what I imagine comes from when she makes herself throw up, if she eats anything. Her mood fluctuates frequently, especially after Dr. Cuvo gave up and disappeared. After he left, she and I grew closer. Janine is beautiful and angry.

Other people seem to see what they want to see in us. However, we know that we're nothing at all like how we see ourselves. Oddly, I see Janine as a lot like myself.

Kristen is a different story. She doesn't cover up

her physical flaws. She shows her bandages. She doesn't even try to hide her face with her hair, always pulling her hair back in a ponytail, as if she was forcing you to look at her face. Ironically, she doesn't look anyone in the eyes. She opens and closes like a broken cabinet that won't shut all of the way unless you slam it hard enough.

I can tell that she's like the others. She sees something in me. She sees something in Janine. She sees something else within herself, but whatever it is, she won't let it go. I can see it too. It's dark, but I can't define it. Kristen scares me and she intrigues me because, unlike Janine, she's not easy to read or understand. She was difficult from the very start.

It seemed like Janine tried to help Kristen feel welcomed. She tried to include Kristen in our group. However, Janine had insisted that Kristen must have disliked us because when Kristen first arrived at Bent Creek, she wouldn't talk to us, nor would she smile. Janine and I made a bet against each other. I bet Janine that Kristen would smile before the end of her first week at Bent Creek and Janine bet that she wouldn't smile. Of course, I won that bet. Janine had to give me her evening snacks for a whole week after I had won the bet! Little did I know, at the time, the loss of that bet wasn't a huge loss for her.

Nonetheless, it was hard work to get Kristen to smile. Eventually, she did smile. After the day that I made her smile, she started to open up more. It seemed to help since we were all in the same group. I didn't want to give up on her. I tried to make her laugh and talk to us about why she is here at Bent Creek, but she seemed too sad to speak about it without getting upset.

On today, of all days, the day before I am

scheduled to be released, this broken and attractively mysterious girl decides to open her mouth and have a real conversation with me. It seems completely unprovoked on my part! At least, I don't think that I've done anything to draw her attention to me.

I am working on a sketch quietly in the commons area on the Adolescent Ward. Drawing helps pass the time. Only one more day until I can go home with my mom and Mom-Mom. I don't want to cause any trouble or lose my temper or let anything trigger me into having a manic episode again. All that I can think about is how much I want to smoke a cigarette. I can't wait until tomorrow! I even asked my mom to bring me a pack of Marlboro's to the hospital so that as soon as I am free, I can take in what I have been craving for over a month!

I haven't told anyone in my group that I am going home because I want to be as inconspicuous about it as I possibly can. I don't want the others to feel badly and then start acting weird around me because I'm leaving.

I don't know. Maybe Kristen senses something in me that gave away my secret because she walks right up to the table where I am sitting and starts talking to me. She surprises me because I am concentrating on drawing straight lines without shaking. I haven't tried to draw since Rocky killed himself. That was a messed up time. Kristen was there, but she hasn't asked me about it. It's a good thing. I don't want to think about it, nor talk about it anymore.

Honestly, I am not prepared to talk about any of this stuff. Really, I'm not ready to open up about what happened with my mom, my dad and Theresa. I'm ready to move past all of that. But Kristen has a way about her that I don't understand. It is the mystery behind her sudden interest that pulls me in and moves me to want to talk to her. When she asks me if I was scared, I may seem to open up to her right away, but in my mind, it seems to take a little more than a minute for me to answer. I am thinking about what she asked and the fact that she is the first person who has asked me if was scared.

Kristen's eyes glisten as she waits for me to speak. I replay her question in my mind.

"Were you scared?" Kristen asked.

When I think about it, I remember everything very clearly. From the moment that I knew that I was in love with her to my dad getting out of prison, and when my mom almost gave up on our family and to Theresa's suicide up to now, this very moment. Here I am, sitting across from Kristen. She's the odd girl that spoke up. Kristen is my inscrutable friend that scares and amazes me. She was the one person who dared to ask me the question that no one, not even Dr. Finch, had ever asked me.

Was I scared?

CHAPTER 2

Sex.

Theresa McElheney was sex.

Of course, I wouldn't have told her that to her face. At least not when I had first met her. I had met her when I was in the seventh grade. Actually, when I was in the seventh grade, I had *not* thought of her that way. I thought that Theresa was a big, mean bully. She seemed to have it out for every boy in the school and I was her most hated toy to push around.

In middle school, I was Theresa's bad habit. She had called me nasty names, pushed me into walls, shoved my head into toilets (yes, in the boys' bathroom), spit in my face, and punched me so hard that she had left me with painful bruises on my chest and face. Theresa used to shove me into the hallway lockers at school and knock me onto the ground. She'd step right over me and never excuse herself as if I was nothing.

On her bad days, when she'd seemed to be most sadistically generous with her affection for me, she'd wait until lunchtime when the cafeteria was full to capacity with our bloodthirsty peers to humiliate me. Our bored and useless colleagues seemed to thrive on the blood sporting entertainment of vicious bullies vs the hunted weak. Lunchroom showdowns seemed to be the antidote to their sickly, mindless wandering through the halls. Perhaps these confrontations helped them get through the anguish of three more periods of torturous schooling. Unfortunately, I was grouped in as part of the bleak veal and doe. At least, that's how Theresa saw me at that time. It's hard to imagine it now, though.

Truthfully, Theresa used to be the legal definition of a bully. You could've gone to any search engine online, typed in her full name and her photo would've been the first to pop up under the image search right next to a picture of a wolf with fresh blood in its teeth.

However, my fondest memories of Theresa are from high school. One time in particular, a time that I could never forget is when she shoved me into the walls inside of my bedroom. She still had that same upper body strength that left me grabbing my chest and throbbing in pain, but this time, I was throbbing much more differently. It wasn't so painful as much as it was crazy and enjoyable. Instead of spitting in my face and leaving me with bruises all over my body, we exchanged spit with our tongues pressed together and left purple and blue marks on each other's hips, necks and shoulders with our mouths.

Why did she used to bully me? I guess it makes sense. Sheep and deer are fine with what they have. They have their freedom in natural surroundings to call a home. I was quiet and I liked to sit alone at lunch. I felt comfortable drawing in my sketchpad with my colored pencils and charcoal pens. I found home in art. That made the hunters, the bullies like Theresa, a fiend for my attention. I was an easy target because I kept my head down so that I could see what I had been drawing. I let myself get lost in the colors of my world. Swirling circles of browns, blues and greens all mixing together to create images that I had hoped to sell one day.

In those days, I didn't pay much attention to the rest of the semi-intelligent existence outside of my own imaginative world of creativity. It's easy to hit someone and humiliate them if they're not looking. With my head down, and my attention on my artwork, Theresa had an opening to hone in on me.

The first time she had hit me, I was trying to draw a replica of Salvador Dali's *City of Drawers*. I had gotten to the intricacy of the knobby breasts that were made of misogynistic, open drawers. The nipples were a bitch to shade in the exact way that Dali had made them. I was just getting to the sweet spot in my shading when I felt Theresa's fists slam into my jaw. My charcoal pencil flew into the air. My sketchpad slid off the lunch table and the sandwich that I had been snacking on, went straight to the floor. She had knocked me clear out of my seat. I fell onto the floor and landed on my back. I had been gasping for air so hard that I felt like I had swallowed bricks. She had knocked the wind out of my lungs.

As I lay on my back, in my bed, Theresa had an opening to pounce on top of me. I was bigger and much stronger because I was a sophomore in high school. However, at that moment, I felt more vulnerable than I did back in the seventh grade. I was naked. She was on top of me, and she was about to do something to me that I never thought would ever happen to me in real life. Sure, I daydreamed about it. I had imagined it happening with the colorfully fun pop star who was always half naked and sensually gyrating in all of her music videos. Never, did I think this would actually happen with a real girl, like Theresa!

When it started to happen, my mind went up to the clouds. It felt like we began to float. I watched every part of Theresa's body move in a rhythmic motion to a silent beat. My whole body seemed to convulse in its own agitation from my body temperature rising. My heart raced as Theresa's hips moved on top of me and handled parts of me that I didn't mind her thrashing around. She was warm, sweet, and rough, but very quiet. To keep my body from bursting to pieces, I clung tightly to my bed sheets, closed my eyes, threw my head back, and opened my mouth. A sound came out of me that I had never heard before. The sound was so shrill and throaty that it actually scared me!

"How did we end up here?" Theresa asked as she put the used condom on my nightstand. Then she sat back on my bed and lit a black cigarette.

I sat still, bewildered by her question.

She laughed and took a light puff of her cigarette and pulled on my boxer shorts.

I wanted to tell her to put on her own underwear because I liked those boxers. They were the only pair of boxers that I had owned with my favorite cartoon character on them.

"You mind?" I asked her, reaching out for my shorts.

Theresa raised an eyebrow at me and kicked my hand.

"Whatever!" Theresa laughed. "Homer likes being up against my ass much better than yours."

Theresa turned away from me to put her shapely butt in my face. There, I saw Homer Simpson's large, white cartoon eyes and smiling yellow face stare and wiggle at me as she gyrated and bumped her hips around teasingly.

Oddly, I felt myself start to rise again and little trickles of whatever was left inside of me began to drip out. Then I turned away from Theresa. It was weird enough that I was seeing Homer's face while it was happening, but even stranger, Theresa was wearing my shorts that I had worn all day before we ended up in my room.

Theresa laughed and pushed me back down on the bed. She jumped on top of me again. From that angle, as she straddled me, she looked and felt better in my shorts than I did. Of course, I was still naked because she deprived me of my underwear. She didn't put on her bra. So, I could see her beautiful arms, soft shoulders and salacious chest. Whatever scars from whatever fights that she used to into didn't bother me. She never did it to herself. Instead, she took it out on me. I didn't mind if this was how she was going to get her frustrations out with me from now on. This kind of shoving around didn't bother me at all.

I looked up at her as she let the ashes from her cigarette fall onto my chest. The ashes burned me on contact. I didn't care. Theresa's black hair fell over her face all wild and crazy. The length of hair was short. The ends went to her neck in the front and it almost lined up with her chin when traced around from the back. She had crazy hair that looked like she couldn't decide between a mohawk and a bob style haircut. It confused the hell out of me, but it was she and I loved her.

Theresa blew the smoke from her cigarette in my face and leaned over me so that her chest would just barely touch my lips. I opened my mouth and closed my eyes. I could smell her sweet sweat from above me. All she had to do was move up just a bit more and lean further in towards my face and I would've tasted her. I pushed my pelvis up against her and immediately regretted it.

"Ugh! Danny!" Theresa jumped up immediately.

Ashes fell to my face and burned me. No matter how much pain I was in from the burns, I couldn't stop what was happening to my body.

"Gross, Daniel!" Theresa whined as she looked down at the mess I had made on her and my shorts.

"What the hell was that all about?" she whined.

Embarrassed, I looked away from her.

"What? Ugh, where's your laundry room?"

"Don't worry about it," I said. "Just leave them on the floor. I'll wash them."

I kept my back towards her because I didn't want her to see the humiliation on my face. My face burned with anger from my stupidity and immaturity.

Theresa's hand felt cool against my shoulder. She pulled me and made me turn towards her. With the cigarette dangling from her mouth, she lay beside me with her face close to mine. Something in my face and in my demeanor gave me away because as soon as she looked at me, she sat up and smacked me on the arm.

"Ow! Sorry! I'm sorry!" I said, sitting up and rubbing my arm.

"Don't tell me," Theresa said, shaking her head.

"Don't tell you what?"

"Don't tell me that this was your first time," Theresa said with a tone that was so scary, I couldn't quite tell if it was safe to admit the truth to her or not.

"Ok..." I choked out, "I *won't* tell you that it was

my first time."

She rose up from my bed and began putting on her blue jeans and a t-shirt that commemorated the anniversary reunion tour of an obscure neo-grunge rock band with whom she was obsessed.

"Wait, are you leaving?" I panicked.

"Does it look like I'm leaving?" She said as she shoved her cigarette between my lips. "I'm going to the bathroom and I'm not going to walk around your house naked just in case your mom is here. Relax! Here, finish this cigarette."

Leaving the fly down on her jeans, showing some bush, she held the bottom of her t-shirt up under her chin, exposing the part of her boobs that was just underneath her nipples as she did the "I Gotta Pee" dance out the door towards the bathroom. She was unscrupulously loud as she chanted, "I gotta go! I gotta go, go, go!" all of the way down the hallway until she was in the bathroom and slammed the door.

My mother wasn't home when we had arrived about a half hour before. Therefore, I wasn't too worried about her being home until I heard heavy footsteps coming towards my door from the opposite direction that Theresa had went in towards the bathroom.

I quickly finished the cigarette and put the butt in a metal ashtray that sat on my dresser. Then I looked down and realized that I was still naked. My clothes, including my messy shorts were thrown about in my room. Not to mention, Theresa's bra and the rest of her underwear were obvious as they hang off the edge of my bed. The used condom sat neatly on top of my nightstand alongside the opened wrapper.

"Daniel!" My mother shouted.

I ran to my bedroom door.

She came around the corner of the hallway and I'm not sure if she got a good look at me, but I closed the door when I saw her coming around the corner.

"What are you doing, Daniel?" Mom said as she banged on my door. "Open this door! I need to talk to you for a minute. It's about Mom-Mom."

Frozen, I stood in front of my closed door with my hands covering my junk as if she could see me.

"Oh, excuse me," I heard Mom say from the other side of the door.

"Yeah, sure," Theresa said as she opened my door.

As the door began to open, I frantically tried to put on my dirty shorts. I fell to the floor, tripping over myself like a clumsy fool. The door swung open. Theresa and Mom looked down at me as I lay with my ass hanging halfway out of the shorts with the big, wet stain on the front of them.

Theresa looked like she wanted to punch me.

Mom threw her head back and laughed.

"Aren't you a site for sick eyes?" Mom laughed.

She reached into her pocket, pulled out a pack of cigarettes, and threw them at me. I caught them just barely between my paws and broke its fall onto my chest.

"You asked for those, right?" Mom asked.

"Uh, yeah. Sure. Thanks," I said.

"You're welcome," Mom said as she stared at Theresa.

Theresa zipped up her jeans and went over to my bed. She grabbed her purse then walked to the door. I just lay there staring up in fright and disbelief at everything that was happening in that moment.

"Theresa!" I called out to her.

"I'll call you," she said as she pushed past my mom and stormed out.

"Theresa, wait!" I shouted.

I scrambled up off the floor and tried to chase after her.

Mom followed behind me as I ran up to the front door. Theresa was already in her car. I shouted out to her once more, but she didn't acknowledge me. She backed out of the driveway and sped up the street.

I went back into my house and slammed the door. Mom stood by the kitchen and smiled at me.

"What?" I growled at her.

"Nothing," she said with her stupid grin. "I didn't say a damn thing."

"You don't have to," I said. "You did enough."

I went back into my room and took off those stupid shorts. I hated Homer. I looked at his retarded, yellow, clownishly simple face before I threw the boxers into the trash can. Then, I took the condom and the wrapper and flushed them both down the toilet. I was surprised to see the wrapper go down with the condom.

My whole body felt hot. Naked, not caring, and filled with an outrageous energy, I went back to my room. I picked up my clothes, the sheets on my bed, my shoes and Theresa's underwear and shoes that she had left behind and threw them all into the washing machine. I poured about a half of what was left of the laundry detergent into the machine and started to wash a load of laundry. Then I grabbed the bottle of bleach and a scrub brush and went to my bedroom. I poured bleach onto everything. Starting with my bed, I doused it with the bleach and I started scrubbing.

My mom came to my room and immediately

covered her nose and her mouth.

"Daniel! What are you doing?" She screamed. "Stop it!"

I heard her, but I couldn't stop. I had to clean. I wanted to get the smell of Theresa and me out of my room. I wanted to get the feeling of frustration and confusion out of my head by cleaning up whatever had just happened between my girlfriend and I.

"Daniel, please!" Mom pleaded. "At least put some clothes on! You're naked! For god's sake, Daniel. You are getting bleach on your skin. Doesn't that burn?"

Burn? What burn? Did she mean the burning sensation I began to feel in my fingers as I scrubbed the very spot where I lost my virginity just a few minutes ago? Or did she mean the burning in my head that seemed to fizzle out every single thought and feeling of agitation and depression from my humiliation?

Whatever she meant, I didn't care. Even when the bleach started to take over my taste buds, close my throat and airway passages and singe my nose buds, I still didn't care. I scrubbed until I could only see black when my eyes rolled to the back of my head. I was sweating thick, clear and white bullets. My arms grew weak and I couldn't see, nor smell anything. I felt my body go limp and I dropped the scrub brush. Just before I hit the floor, someone caught me in their arms.

While I was being dragged on the hardwood floors by whoever caught me, I heard Mom sobbing.

She cried, "Thank you for coming over. I didn't know what else to do or who to call. He just wouldn't stop throwing bleach everywhere and cleaning his room. Thank goodness, he just passed out *this time*. When he starts cleaning, it could last for hours before he'd tire himself out. I hate it when he gets like this. He scares the hell out of me. The last time he had a manic episode, he almost set the whole damn house on fire!

"I don't know what to do, Tom. I just don't know what to do with him. I'm tired of dealing with him alone. Next time, I don't know what he'll do. He could burn down my home or he could bleach everything and destroy it all. His episodes are getting more unpredictable. His medicine doesn't do anything. His doctor is an idiot because I keep telling him that those antidepressants are making him act out even more than before he was taking them. What am I supposed to do, Tom? What am I going to do if I have to pull momma out of the nursing home and she has to come live here with us? I can't have her around him when he's acting insane."

Even though I was passed out, I could still hear her crying as well as everything that she was saying.

"Is he going to be alright?" Mom finally asked.

CHAPTER 3

"He will be fine," I heard Tom declare.

As if I couldn't be more humiliated, Mom decided to call over our neighbor, Tom Lawrence. Tom was the only other person in my life that was close to a dad. My real dad was locked up a few years prior. Tom lived next door to us and he helped mom with repairs around the house and the heavy yard work. I wasn't the kind of person who actually enjoyed pulling tree stumps and chopping wood. However, I didn't mind raking the leaves and cutting the grass to earn some cash for cigarettes. That's why mom had brought the pack for me before that prior episode.

Unfortunately, my episodes seemed to be occurring more frequently and we didn't seem to understand it at the time. Despite my frequent manic episodes, I did take my medicine.

I woke up on the couch, covered in three quilts. Sweat dripped down from my head to my chest. I tried to sit up and immediately a heavy weight in my head dropped down my whole body and I fell right back down onto the couch. My hair stuck to my shoulders and my back from the sweat. I needed to take a shower.

"Mom!" I shouted.

Tom walked up and stood beside me with a glass

of ice water. I reached out and swiped it away.

"Mom!" I called out again.

I pushed the covers off my body and covered my eyes with my hands. I heard Tom sigh. He sat down beside me on the couch. Mom came into the living room with smoke billowing all around her. She was smoking *my cigarettes*. I could tell that she was smoking out of stress because she had a tendency to chain smoke whenever I'd have an episode. She was holding a black bag. I knew why she had that bag and it made me angry.

"I've got your insulin right here, Daniel," my mom said. She sounded sad and yet so proud of herself for thinking to bring me insulin. Her sincerity made me feel a bit guilty.

I reached out to her. She leaned forward to give me the black bag. However, I snatched the cigarette that she had hanging out of her mouth and before she could try to take it back, I put it my mouth and took a long, heavy drag that disintegrated most of it. By the time I took a breath away from the nicotine, all that was left was dangling ashes and a butt.

Tom laughed and said, "It looks like you're feeling better."

When I started to answer, I coughed a cloud of smoke out. I nodded and gave him a thumb up. But no, seriously, I needed my insulin. I sat up slowly this time and put the cigarette in the ashtray that sat on the coffee table.

"Here you go, Daniel," Mom said, handing over the black bag.

I took the bag from my mom and began my insulin ritual. First, I start by checking my blood sugar levels. It's just a prick to the finger, a little blood goes into a machine and a magic number pops up on the screen. Nothing above 120 is good. The machine read 280. That means that I need to inject myself with insulin. I prepared the syringe and loaded it up with the insulin then tapped on the needle to get the air bubbles out. I stared at the needle, long, thin and horrifyingly sharp.

Mom's eyes seemed, always, to tear up a bit whenever she had to watch me take my insulin. She's gotten better about it. However, when we first found out that I had diabetes I was 12 years old and Mom freaked out about it. She cried every time I had to take my medicine. Mom used to have to give me my shots. It was painful and we wouldn't always get it right because she was scared to stick me. I had to learn to do it myself because she'd hurt me more than she actually helped me. Her fear and guilt made things worse. Mom learned to let me take care of it myself. And she looked away when I had to stick myself.

Funny, the manly and tough Tom decided to watch and yet he still flinched.

"You took quite a spill there," Tom said after clearing his throat. "You know kid, you have to be more careful. When you feel like you're getting upset, go for a walk, talk to your mom or me. I'm next door if you want to talk. Throwing fits and getting everything all covered up in bleach isn't going to help you feel better. Besides, you don't want to scare your mom like that again. Do you?"

It was just like Tom to start with the obvious. Instead of just getting to the point, he had a way of working his way up to it with little comments that turned into discussions, which were more like lectures, until finally he would come right out with what he actually wanted to say. Tom got on my nerves when he kept going on and on. He was just like a father or an old grandpa that I never really had.

My high blood sugar levels made me feel dizzy. It wasn't just because I was still upset. Moreover, I felt like something was coming. Tom was still there, even though I was calm and seemed to be doing better. He didn't really hang around like this unless my mom asked him to stay.

"You understand what I'm saying?" Tom asked me.

Effortlessly, I stuck the needle into my right upper thigh and watched Tom cringe. I grinned and nodded at him. My mom gave Tom a sympathetic look.

It bugged me how they both were lingering around me as they waited for me to say or do something. The way they kept staring at me and at each other pinched a nerve. I took the needle out of my thigh when all of the insulin had been injected into me.

"Are you feeling better?" Tom asked.

"If only it would work that fast," Mom chuckled, answering for me.

I couldn't take it anymore.

"Okay, what's going on?" I asked.

"What do you mean, Daniel?" Tom asked.

Mom had a look on her face that made me want to scream at her just to tell me. I stared up at her, giving her a look that begged her to open her mouth and speak.

"Well, I might as well tell you," Mom said as she took a seat beside Tom on the opposite side of him.

It was almost as if she wanted to be as far away from me as possible. She leaned away from Tom and me and rested her elbow on the arm of the sofa, leaned against it and took a deep breath with her eyes closed. Finally gaining her composure, mom began, "Mom-Mom is coming to stay with us."

When she said "Mom-Mom", I wasn't sure of whom she was talking about at first. Her mother and father are dead. They had died before I was born. Then I remembered that my biological father's mother was still alive. I hadn't seen Mom-Mom since my father had been incarcerated.

"Okay," I said.

Mom stayed quiet and looked at Tom. She seemed confused, as if she was expecting me to say more.

"Well, is that okay with you?" Mom asked.

"I said 'okay'," I tried to make it clear to her.

Mom still seemed to be confused.

"What more do you want me to say, Mom?"

"Uh, I guess, nothing...I mean...Tom? You want to...?"

Tom nervously pulled the covers over my lap to cover me up. I guess my nakedness suddenly bothered him. Mom and I had very little boundaries, which my psychiatrist had suggested was a problem. Tom must have been the one who put all of those blankets over me. I felt disgusting from how much I was sweating. I just wanted to take a shower and for them to leave me alone.

"What your mother is trying to say is that your grandma is coming to live with you. There will be some major changes around here. For one thing, you have to help out more. You can't throw tantrums like the one you had today. Take your medicine regularly. No girls in the house. And you can't walk around naked like that. That's very inappropriate and disrespectful. Your grandma doesn't need to have all of that going on around her. She is in a very delicate-"

"AAAAAAH!" I yelled until he finally stopped talking.

I slammed my fist in to the palm of my hand and yelled loudly in Tom's face. I didn't say anything, I just yelled out. Tom and my mom stared at me wide-eyed and silent.

Calmly, I picked up the half pack of Marlboro's off the coffee table. Half of it had already been smoked. Then I put a cigarette in my mouth and lit it.

"Daniel, I-"

"AH!" I shouted at mom before she could go on. She shut up.

"I feel sick right now. I'm going to take a shower."

I threw the heavy blankets off my lap and stood up.

"Jesus Christ," Tom sighed and looked away from me.

Mom shook her head in disapproval and lit another cigarette.

I went to the bathroom, finished smoking my cigarette and flushed the butt down the toilet. Then I got into the shower. As soon as the hot water hit my skin, I fell to my knees. All I could think about was Theresa and what had happened between us. What did it mean? What we did, would it happen again? Was she my girlfriend? Did she hate me?

Theresa said that she'd call, but I didn't give her my number. I had to clean myself up and try to get my head straight so that I could go out and find her. There was no way that I would get through the night without talking to her.

Earlier that day, at school, I had heard about a party at some kid named Ryan's house. Theresa was friends with Ryan. Surely, she'd be at his party. I didn't care much for Ryan's parties. Mostly, because he was a spoiled rich kid from school whose parents were always on vacation or out of town on business trips. Affluent people. When they left him, alone he took out his rage on his parents by opening the doors of their home to strangers. This is what made Ryan popular. He didn't have anything else going for him except the fact that he had money and a huge house with no parents. Kids at school wanted a place to chill and have sex, fight and trash, smoke and drink until they threw up everywhere and on everything.

Ryan was most popular for his drug intense parties. His parties almost never got as wild as most of the others I heard about because everyone would get so high that people were too low to trash anything. I had heard that there was more sex and drinking at his parties than there was fighting. So, I didn't think that it would do much harm to go looking for Theresa at Ryan's house.

After a long nap in the shower, I felt a little less lightheaded. I got dressed in a clean pair of jeans, a collared shirt and my favorite black hoodie. As I passed mom in the living room, I felt her cold stare. She lay on the couch on top of the blankets that Tom had thrown over me. Tom was gone.

I grabbed the keys to her car from off the bookshelf that hardly shelved any books. Mom sat up and threw something at me. Whatever it was, it felt weird and it bounced right off my head.

"What the-?"

"Where do you think you're going?" Mom yelled.

"Mom," I whined. "Why'd you throw a soda can at me?"

"Stop crying," she said. "It's an empty can. Where do you think you're going with my car keys?"

"I'm going to the store," I lied. "You smoked all of the cigarettes. I just want to get some more."

"Oh," Mom said as she calmly lay back down. "Go to the store and come right back. We're not finished talking about Mom-Mom."

"Sure, okay," I said and walked out the door.

I hurried out the door in case mom decided to ask me to grab more things from the store. I had no intention of going to the store. Although, I did plan to get more cigarettes, I had hoped to get some from Ryan or someone at the party.

As I drove to Ryan's house, I couldn't stop thinking about Theresa and all of the things that we did with each other that afternoon. I had no idea that we'd end up back at my place after school. During our lunch period on that day, she came up to me and put her arm around me. She asked me questions about myself and genuinely showed an interest in me. We had been talking a few weeks prior to that day, but this was the first day she had actually touched me without any intent on hurting me. Or so I thought...

When she left, I had no idea where we stood. She left too suddenly. We hadn't had a chance to talk about what kind of relationship we would have or even if we would do it again. If she were my girlfriend, then I would hope that we would do it again. Perhaps it would be less awkward and more romantic. Maybe she'd let me prove myself to her. Show her that I'm not stupid. I wanted to be someone that she could like, even fall in love with and definitely want to have sex with again.

It was mom's fault anyway. If she hadn't barged in

and scared Theresa, then we would have probably been able to do it again and talk about having a relationship. It didn't matter. I was pretty sure that Theresa was my girlfriend. She had to be because, as far as I was concerned, I already loved her.

When I arrived at Ryan's house, I parked a few houses down from his home where the sound of vintage dub-step pulsated. I walked up to Ryan's upper middle class brick mansion. It looked bigger when I stood right in front of it, up close. The size of his home intimidated me because I lived in a one story flat home with less than 1000 square feet to the structure. Ryan's house was gigantic and easily stood at five levels high. I wondered how many bedrooms his place had, let alone the square feet.

Kids from my school who I recognized, but I didn't really know all that well, stretched out on the front lawn under pillows of smoke that smelled like fresh skunk. I waved the smoke away from my face as I approached the front door. The door was wide open. The ceiling lights inside were turned off, giving the living room and corridors a dark, club scene ambiance. Black lights that hung on the walls and sat on top of tables made everyone who was wearing white and light colors look like they were neon colored. I had to blink my eyes to adjust to the change in the light and contrast.

Suddenly, two girls approached me. Both of them glowed like a photonegative. Their skin looked dark in contrast to their luminescent white teeth and hair, brightly colored tight white shirts, and the neon green, yellow and blue glow sticks that accessorized their wrists, necks and hair. One of the girls reached up and rubbed the back of my neck. When she opened her mouth to speak, I saw a smaller glow stick inside of her mouth. The glow stick illuminated her teeth in bright neon green. She smiled widely and open-mouthed. Her friend began to touch my chest. As she opened her mouth and smiled, I saw that she had a red, glowing tongue ring.

I felt confused.

The girl with the glowing green mouth slowly ran her hand up and down my neck. She leaned into my ear and whispered, "I'm so fucking high right now. I want you."

"Me too," her friend joined in.

Well, that explained why these two illuminating neon nymphs were molesting me. They grew more aggressive with their touching, moving their hands lower down my back and my pelvic area. I quickly removed their hands and leaned away from them. They looked confused and offended.

"What's wrong with you?" Green Mouth asked.

"Yeah," Red Mouth whined. "What's wrong? Do you need something to loosen you up?"

Green Mouth held out a small, white and oval shaped pill to me in the palm of her hand.

"No," I laughed. I couldn't help it. I had to laugh at this bizarre situation.

"It's just an X," Red Mouth pushed.

"Or we have PushKing, if you prefer," squeaked Green Mouth.

I waved both of them off and tried to walk away, but Red Mouth and Green Mouth blocked my path.

"Have you seen Theresa?" I said as I began to grow impatient.

"Who?" Red Mouth shouted while rolling her eyes.

"Theresa McElheney!" I shouted back at her.

"What about her?" Green Mouth asked, seemingly annoyed.

"Have you seen her?" I repeated.

The two girls didn't seem interested in me anymore as they pulled vials of white containers from their bras. Green Mouth sprinkled white powder on her hand and sniffed it through her nostrils. Red Mouth did the same. They looked back up at me with wide eyes and their smiles returned.

"Yeah, sure," said Red Mouth. "She's out back with Ryan and those guys."

"Want us to take you to her?" Green Mouth asked.

Before I could answer, they both grabbed a hold of my arms and dragged me through the living room full of drugged out, dazed and euphorically crazed partygoers.

"You should really try some of this," Green Mouth encouraged me as she held out the white vial. She pushed it close to my face.

"No thanks," I pushed it away.

She pouted and placed the vial to her nostrils and sniffed more of the white powder. She smiled again, tucked the vial away into her bosom, and shrugged her shoulders.

In the kitchen, dim track lights on the ceiling made an ambient, warm light around the room. The first person that I saw in the kitchen was McKayla Flemming. McKayla was a short girl with dark hair and large beady eyes. She stood at the elegant electrical, touch screen stove, stirring a large pot that released lots of steam and a fetid smell. She looked like a little witch standing over that large pot, stirring like a mad woman. I remembered her from my chemistry class. She was Dr. Flemming's daughter. Dr. Flemming used to be our health teacher in the 9th grade. Now, he's head master of our school. His new position seemed to put McKayla in the popular and untouchable group, with kids such as Ryan and Rex King, the captain of our school's soccer team.

As McKayla stirred the stinking contents in the pot, other guys and girls stood around her with cups in their hands and stared at her while she spoke in a low, calm voice. I could hear her as we walked passed them. The sickening smell grew stronger.

"The key to making it potent is the chemical solution," she instructed as she poured black liquid from an unlabeled bottle into the pot. "You don't want to put in too much, but just enough so that it mixes well with the Pseudoephedrine."

"Why does it smell like that?" A guy with ginger red hair and bugged out eyes asked as he stuck his face closer to the pot.

She waved him away and said, "That's just the chemicals mixing. Give it a minute. The smell won't matter when it's in your system. You won't even be thinking about that while you're tripping."

I wiped my eyes from the strong smell and the smoke. I almost couldn't stand it. I was relieved when we walked into the spacious back yard. The feel of the outside air in my lungs provided relief. I coughed until I could get the rancid tastes and smell of raw chemicals out of my throat and nose. Once I caught my breath, I looked out at the back yard in search of Theresa. I looked at the Olympic sized rectangular pool that had a few people in it, but mostly everyone was chilling off to the side in lawn chairs. I searched the lawn chairs, the gazebo, and the outdoor bar where Ryan's best friend, Logan, was mixing drinks and serving them up in paper cups. He was obviously drunk. He mixed light liquor with dark alcohol. He even poured white rum into a cup of beer and called it a Logan Cock & Tail. I walked away from the bar when Logan tried to make me drink it. I let Green Mouth and Red Mouth take the drink for me. I left them at the bar hut with Logan and his dirty concoctions and walked towards the back.

As I walked around the back, I could hear people laughing and the sound of water splashing. The laughs were coming from Ryan and the sounds of splashing water came from him tossing water around in his hot tub. He splashed water on Theresa. She was topless, only dressed in a pair of black panties. She splashed around in the hot tub with Ryan and two other guys who I did not recognize. They looked too old to be from my school. The older looking guy had a tattoo across his chest that read *Too Young Too Die And Too Old To Care* and the other guy had a full on beard that looked like a glued pile of pubes stuck to his square, hard face. He kept his long, blonde hair back in a bun. Theresa tried to avoid Ryan's water attacks by wrapping her arms around the bun head man and pressing her face into his foul looking beard and her bare breasted chest into his.

"Theresa!" I shouted.

Theresa looked up and at first; it looked like she didn't recognize me. She didn't seem to know who called out to her. I realized that I was standing in the shadows at the rear of the bar hut. I stood in the darkness, staring at them looking like I was some kind of creeper.

"Who is that?" Ryan called out.

I stepped into the light. Theresa gasped then began laughing.

"Are you serious?" Ryan asked, laughing along

with Theresa.

"Who the hell is this guy?" Man Bun asked.

His older friend stepped out of the hot tub with a beer in his hand and approached me with his chest puffed out.

"Who are you? What do you want with Theresa?"

I stayed quiet and looked at, no, glared at Theresa. I reached out to her.

"Come on, Theresa," I said. I tried to keep my voice calm.

Theresa let go of Man Bun and started to step out of the hot tub until Man Bun grabbed her wrist. She stopped and looked at him.

"She's not going with you," Man Bun said.

"She wants to stay with us," the older, tattooed guy growled at me.

"C'mon," Ryan tried to reason. "It's okay. Let's all just chill out. Theresa, are you staying with us?"

"Of course she's staying with us," Man Bun demanded. He pulled Theresa close to him and wrapped her arms around him. It made her breasts press up against his chest again.

"She was just about to give us some head," the older guy said with a nasty grin. His stupid smile exposed his discolored and crooked front teeth. He rubbed the tattoo on his chest and spit at me. His loogie missed my foot by an inch.

Theresa pulled away from Man Bun and whimpered when he wouldn't let her go. I jumped forward and reached out to Theresa again. This time I got a hold of her arm. Man Bun shoved me away and I stumbled back. Ryan got between us when I regained my balance.

"No," Ryan scolded. "We are not doing this. I will shut this whole thing down if anyone starts fighting." Ryan turned to Theresa. "Theresa, you okay?"

Theresa folded her arms across her chest, covering her breasts as she stepped out of the hot tub. She nodded silently at Ryan.

Ryan nodded back at her and looked at Man Bun and his older friend.

He asked, "Are we cool, guys?"

Man Bun gave Theresa the cold stare. His friend finished off his beer and began to walk away, heading back towards the front of the bar hut.

"This party is lame," he complained as he stormed off. "Stupid high school bitch."

Man Bun fussed as he settled back into the hot tub with Ryan, "I don't want a whore, anyway."

Theresa didn't look fazed by their comments. Ryan lit a pipe that I was sure was filled with ganja and he and Man Bun smoked. Theresa stormed past me. I followed behind her and took off my hoodie. When I caught up with her near the pool, I tried to put my hoodie around her shoulders. She pushed me away from her and kept walking.

"Theresa, stop!" I said to her.

"Leave me alone," she demanded.

"No," I pressed on.

"What are you doing here, Danny?" She seemed upset.

"I came to see you," I replied. "Why else would I come here?" I tried to give her my hoodie again, but she continued to push me away.

"Are you crazy?" she shouted.

"Am I crazy? I'm not the one walking around

outside half naked, in a pair of thongs. Where are your clothes?"

"Who do you think you are?"

Theresa stopped walking. She shoved me. I stumbled back, bumped up against a swing set, and realized that we were way past the pool, the gazebo and the house. Somehow, we'd made our way far away from everyone and the party. Still on Ryan's huge property, we were on the left side of his house, somewhere between the house and a brown fence. On the other side of the fence, I could see windows to Ryan's neighbor's attic. A chimney top stood above the attic.

"You don't get to come out here and judge me! I didn't ask you to rescue me! Really, Danny? Who do you think you are?"

"I thought that I was your..." my voice failed me.

"What?"

"I mean, I thought that I...today, ya know when we...I mean. Theresa..." I couldn't find the right words to tell her that I loved her.

Theresa could see it in my eyes. Her angry demeanor seemed to melt away as she observed me as I struggled to express myself. She stepped closer to me and raised her hand. I flinched and held up my hoodie to protect my face. I thought that she was going to hit me. Instead, she took my hoodie away from me. When I looked back up at her, she had put on the hoodie and wrapped her arms around her chest, hugged herself and snuggled into my jacket. It looked oversized on her. She smiled at me.

"Thanks, Danny. It's getting cold out here," she said.

"No problem," I told her.

Theresa sat down on one of the swings and I stood up beside her. She began lightly pushing herself on the swing. I wanted to wrap my arms around her and warm her up more because she didn't have shoes on her feet, nor pants pulled up around her waist. I was too nervous to try to grab her while she was swinging.

"I wasn't really going to do it," Theresa said, matter-of-factually.

"Do what?" I asked.

"I wasn't going to go down on all of those guys. Especially not Ryan. Ugh!" She shook her head and stuck out her tongue. She seemed disgusted by the thought of it.

"That old guy sure thought that you were going to do it," I said.

Theresa stopped swinging and looked up at me.

"A lot of people *think* that I do a lot of things."

"Is that because you do most of the things that they think you do?"

"Sometimes," she admitted. "Other times, I *do* want them to think that I do those things, even when I don't."

"Why would you want people to think that about you?"

"Because," she said as she put her bare feet on top of both of my feet, perhaps to warm them. "It's better people think something of me, whether it's true or not, rather than they don't think anything of me at all. I find that I make more of an impact when I allow them to think of me as someone that they don't think they are."

"What are they, if you're not like them?"

"They're hypocrites!"

I was shocked at her response.

"How so?"

"Think about it," she said. "Most of these people here will smoke or whatever and end up sleeping with someone else here who may or may not be their boyfriend or girlfriend. Tomorrow, they'll pretend as if nothing happened. Then they'll talk about me and say how I hooked up with Ryan and his cousins in the hot tub, but I won't deny it even though I didn't do it. Believe me, there will be someone who will say that they saw me do it just so that they won't have to talk about whom they were cheating. It's gross how they'll do it, talk about me and lie, but I don't care. They're the ones who care about what other people are doing when they need to worry about themselves. I don't mind it, though, because I know that I have no problem doing whatever I want with whoever I want and I won't be a hypocrite like all of them."

Silently, I listened to her speak her mind. She spoke strongly and seemed confident in herself and who she was. I wasn't mad at her. Actually, I was more amazed by her boldness and freedom to be herself without caring what other people said about her.

"Do you think that makes me weird?"

Theresa looked to me for a response. I smiled at her.

"No," I assured her. "You're not weird because of what you said."

There was only one thing that was on my mind and I was sure of it.

"I think you're kinda awesome," I confessed.

Theresa gently punched me in the chest.

"Shut up," she said with a smile.

"No, really," I said. I bent down to her level on the

swing so that she could see my face as I spoke to her. "You're beautiful! You're strong and you know who you are. No one can tell you how to be or what to do. I love that about you."

"You *love* that about me?"

"Yes," I said. "That's why I want you to be my girlfriend."

"What? No." Theresa shook her head and looked away from me.

"Come on, Theresa. I really like you and I think that you like me. Today was fun. Wasn't it?"

"Yeah, it was, but..."

"Then, be my girlfriend. Try it for a week, and if you don't like me, you can dump me and break my heart. But at least give me a chance before you do it now."

Theresa turned back around, leaned in towards me and grabbed my face with both of her hands. She squeezed my cheeks tightly, causing my lips to pucker up and make a fish face.

"OK, *Danny Boy*," she said with a slight grin.

I smiled at her nickname for me. I liked it. It was new and cute. She pulled my face close to hers and kissed me. I wrapped my arms around her and pulled her close to me. I gripped her by the hips and lifted her off the swing as I pulled her closer. I felt her shiver in my arms. We kissed each other, deeply. I lifted her up with my legs and she wrapped her legs around my waist. I held her up, in my arms and secured her hips up against me by caressing her strongly with my hands underneath her. Theresa pulled her lips away from my mouth to breathe. Her eyes remained closed as she deeply inhaled and exhaled. She smiled as she opened her beautiful, yet piercing eyes. Her stare was seductive and it awakened every part of me that made me aware that I was a man who was in love with this girl. Of course, I wouldn't admit that to her yet.

Looking at me with her stupidly passionate stare, she said, "Danny, do you want to take me home?"

"You want to go home, now?" I asked feeling disappointed.

"Do you want to take me back to your house?" she asked.

I thought about my mom, Tom, that weird conversation he tried to have with me, and the bleach incident. At the risk of being asked if I was crazy again, I shook my head.

"What about your house?" I asked.

"No!" Theresa said abruptly.

"Okay. What do you want to do?"

"I think I know a place where we can go."

"Really? Where?" I became excited again.

"Carry me to your car and I'll show you."

"Carry you?"

"Yes. Come on!"

"Okay, you asked for it!" I lifted Theresa up higher and tossed her onto my shoulder. She squeaked and laughed.

"Oh, Danny, you're so strong!" she exclaimed, sarcastically.

While I ran with Theresa on my shoulders, she laughed hysterically. I laughed as she hit me and playfully screamed out to the world that I was kidnapping her. No one seemed bothered by us as I ran by the lawn and down the street towards my car. The feeling of having Theresa in my arms again was wonderful. She and I were together and she said that she'd be my girlfriend. I wanted us to be like that, laughing, having fun, kissing and making love. In that moment, I thought that nothing would ever change between us. At least, that is what I hoped.

CHAPTER 4

Drawing relaxes me.

There was only one box of crayons and a drawing pad filled with multi-colored construction paper. I made use of those tools because it was all that I had to work with. Theresa lay beside me on the floor. She snored while she slept. Her wild hair lay spread out and strewn across her face. I couldn't draw her likeness if I wanted to. I didn't want to draw her, though. I only drew the faces of strangers. I was more comfortable drawing people that I didn't know rather than people that I already knew and had an attachment to. It felt too personal. When I draw people, it makes me see things. And sometimes I see things that I don't care to see in them. Sometimes it hurts me in a way that I can't describe. If I don't really know them, then I don't have to care anymore after I finish drawing them. It doesn't hurt me to draw strangers.

With a black crayon, I began to sketch out the living room where we had just made love. It was inside of a strange house that I had never seen before. Theresa had found a white sheet in one of the bedrooms inside of the seemingly uninhabited, three bedrooms, and one-story house. She had broken in through a window that she must have known had been unlocked. Then she let me in through the front door. The house still had furniture in it like the family that had once lived there was going to come back from a long vacation. However, everything seemed to have been abandoned a long time ago because the furniture was dusty and it had an empty house smell. There wasn't the smell of human must, the sweat of life, or the scent of living spirits. There was no sense of warmth that comes with a home that is filled with an active force of existence. In fact, the place seemed spooky and gave me a creepy vibe due to the house's soullessness.

Theresa stirred in her sleep. Every time she moved, I stopped drawing to look at her just in case she woke up. I froze when she let out a whimper that sounded more like a cat meowing. She looked up at me through half closed eyes and let out a low "meow-meow".

"What?" I whispered.

She snorted, closed her eyes and put her head back down on the floor. She didn't make another sound. I assumed that she went back to dream land where no doubt she was licking her paws and enjoying a bowl of milk.

When my black crayon was worn down, I looked through the box of mostly broken and melted colors of wax to see what I could find to work with. There wasn't much. I looked at my drawing and frowned. I had almost captured the whole of the living room, but I was missing the cold, ash-filled fireplace and the Dust Bunny Apartments aka the empty bookshelf that was beside the fireplace.

I stood up and headed down a long hallway that lead me back to the bedroom where I originally found the box of crayons and construction paper. Walking down those halls made me shiver. The home had once belonged to somebody. What happened to them? I had no idea. It couldn't have been good, though. At least I didn't feel like something good had happened since the hairs on the back of my neck stood up as I walked deeper into the hallway.

I pushed open the bedroom door, slowly. I tried not to feel the cold draft or smell the stale air around me that came with opening that door. A little girl's frilly daybed sat near a window with lace sheets and dusty white pillows propped up around deserted teddy bears and decaying porcelain dolls. Beyond the horror of the room, I found myself surrounded by the essence of a typical suburban little girl's life. I began to wander around the room in search of more crayons, a pencil, or an ink pen, anything to finish my drawing.

I couldn't sleep after the last time we were inside of each other. Somehow, she'd grown tired and worn out after a few times, but I remained awake. I could feel a burst of energy rising within me. I knew what was coming, but I didn't want to think about it.

I enjoyed the feeling I got when I had my energy boosts. My doctor calls it a manic episode, but I used to call it *happiness*. Theresa did that to me. She brought me happiness. The energy that she gave me made me feel like there was no such thing as depression. There was no such thing as low moods and high blood sugar levels. You know, they were the things that kept me down. Theresa was my medicine.

Something caught my attention in that ghost of a little girl's bedroom. It was her closet. The door was pushed partially open and there were a few dresses on the floor. I opened the closet door a little more and saw three dresses; all of them colored in pastels, lay on the floor, turned inside out and covered in dirt. I wanted to pick the dresses up and put them on hangers, but I thought about how crazy that would seem to the people who lived here. They'd come home and suddenly things would be out of place. It's not enough that I used up the little girl's crayons and drew in her art journal. I decided to leave things as they were as I continued to search for another box of crayons.

The art on her walls were the definition of "girly-girl". She had paintings of horses and a large, blue Japanese style fan with hints of gold, brown and red hanging near her white armoire and vanity dresser. There were only two photographs hanging on the wall. They caught my attention. The photos weren't of popular singers and actors or anything like that.

The first photo was of a picture perfect family. The photograph was of a family of four people: An older man and woman, perhaps in their late thirties or early forties, a young man with golden blond hair and lean build, seemingly in his late teens and a little blond girl who looked no more than ten years old. The family of four posed with smiles, dressed in their Sunday's best, while standing in front of a sign that I couldn't read. The words were blurry, but I could tell that it was some sort of religious institution. The building was made of brick. It didn't have any windows. Two white pillars stood in front of the building underneath an awning made of concrete. Behind the pillars stood a welcoming set of double, wide doors that seemed to whisper, "come to me and you shall be free". I looked at the area surrounding the family. There was a parking lot filled with cars and other people dressed in formal clothing.

Moving on to the other photo that hung on the wall, I ran my index finger across the vanity of the little girl's dresser. It was a photo of whom I imagined was the little girl and her family. Except, the little girl, wasn't a little girl anymore. She looked to be in her early teens. Her hair was more golden brown than it was blonde. The boy from the previous photo looked to be in his later teens, if not early twenties. The mother and father still looked the same, except they had a few more strands of gray in their hair. The family posed close together with the mother and father, in the background smiling with their hands pressed to the shoulders of the boy and the girl as they posed in front of the parents. They were all dressed in swimsuits and flip-flops.

The family of four looked happy. All of them were smiling and touching each other in some way, with their hands placed upon a shoulder, as they pressed close to each other. The sun illuminated their faces and seemed to caress them with a sense of relaxation and joy. I realized it must've been a family vacation photo to some place exotic and beautiful like Hawaii or Fiji as I observed the clear, blue ocean behind them and the diamond-like white sands beneath their tanned feet.

Suddenly, I felt like I was intruding on this ghost family. For sure, I thought that the little girl in the photo was going to show her restless spirit. Blood would spew from her mouth. She'd raise her undead, cold, gray hands and stretch them out to me. Her hair would rise up from static energy that she sucked from the room like the jilted Medusa. She'd scream at me for disturbing her haunted haven in a horrifying shrill voice and devour me with one, darkly hollow, open-mouthed swallow.

I forgot about the crayons and quickly walked back

towards the living room. When I saw Theresa sitting up, topless and staring at me with an expression on her face that I was not quite used to yet, I stopped in my tracks.

"What?" I asked.

Theresa shrugged. "I thought you left," she said.

"How can I leave?" I asked her. "My shorts are right beside you."

"Commando?"

"Okay," I said, "But so are my jeans."

Theresa opened her eyes widely as if she had just realized that I was standing in front of her completely naked.

"How could I go anywhere like this?" I asked her as I walked up to her and began to slide on my shorts. "I don't have a thing for exposing in public." I laughed.

Theresa snorted.

"I went to look for a pencil or something," I explained.

"Why?" Theresa asked.

I held up the drawing pad and showed her my incomplete drawing of the living room.

"No fireplace. No bookshelf. You're bad at this," Theresa said, seemingly unimpressed.

"No," I said snatching the drawing away, a bit offended. "I ran out of black crayon."

"Then use another color," she suggested.

I ripped the drawing out of the drawing pad and began to ball it up.

"You can't do that! It doesn't work that way!" I felt myself getting upset.

"Okay! Alright!" Theresa must've sensed it. She continued, "I get it. You like to have it just right."

"Yeah," I said.

She pushed my wild curls out of my face and touched her fingertips to my right temple. She gave my head a slight push and tried to make eye contact with me, but I turned away from her.

"There's nothing wrong with that," she said.

I turned back around to look at her. Made sure she was not messing with me.

"No, that's okay, Danny Boy. I like that about you. I like that you have a way about you. You like things to be some kind of right. Without the unknown *chaos*."

Chaos...

She got me. Theresa knew and I didn't even have to tell her. She didn't seem bothered by the fact that I was a bit off in a way about things.

"Come with me," she said as she stood up.

She slipped my t-shirt over her head and pulled it on over herself. I cringed a little, but I let it go as she took my hand. She led me down the hallway and into the second bedroom that I had not been in yet. The room was painted blue and it had a wallpaper border that lined the top of the walls just below the ceiling. The white wallpaper border design was made up of baseballs, bats and The Atlanta Braves' team logo. The border lined the whole room in its entirety. A bunk bed stood out of place in the center of the room. I thought that was weird. There were two beanbags randomly propped in a corner of the room. A full-length body mirror hung on the closed closet door. A small computer desk sat in the corner. A lamp in the shape of a baseball sat on top of the desk. Theresa turned that lamp on and the room brightened up. She opened the desk drawer as if she knew exactly what she was looking for. She pulled out a number two lead pencil and, to my surprise, a black charcoal pencil. She held the utensils out to me.

"Will this work?" Theresa asked with a seductive smile.

I quickly snatched the pencils from her.

She looked happily satisfied with herself.

Before we headed back to the living room, Theresa shut off the lamp. As we walked to the living room, I noticed her shapeliness and how it affected my t-shirt. I did not want to say anything, but...

"You like wearing my clothes, don't you?"

Theresa laughed. "Yeah. What's wrong with it?" She plopped back down on the floor and crossed her legs.

I shook my head and remained calm. "Nothing."

"Are you going to finish drawing the living room?" she asked.

I smiled at her and nodded. It flattered me that she was interested in what I was drawing and if I was going to finish.

"I only started drawing because you fell asleep on me," I told her.

"OK, Danny Boy," she sighed, "We can't all be Gladiators."

"What does that mean?" I chuckled as I pressed the charcoal pencil to the drawing pad and began to draw the outline of the old fireplace.

"Nothing," she sighed.

I didn't want to ruin the moment. So, I let it go.

"Don't you want to know about this place?" Theresa asked.

I stopped drawing for a moment. Did she know this place? I was curious.

"Sure..." I tried not to sound too interested.

"Once upon a time," she paused and looked at me

with a wild grin that I couldn't quite understand, and it scared me a little. "This house belonged to a family."

"Really?" I mean, obviously.

"Yes, really!" she shouted as she smacked my right arm. Her blow made me jerk forward and I quickly lifted my hand with the pencil from the paper. Luckily, I wasn't drawing with my right hand at the moment. I learned not to rub the spot where she caused me pain. When I did that, it only made her want to abuse me more.

"Anyway," she continued, "A family once lived here. It was a nice family. Like *church* kind of nice. And there was a mom, a dad, a son, and a daughter. They were sorta, kinda happy, too, believe it or not."

"Hmm," I mouthed as I bit on my bottom lip and started shading in the shadows of the fireplace's cold, dark and gray corners.

"The father was a laborer. He was a hard working man. The mother was a home-maker. She was all about taking care of her children and her home. The brother was a skilled sportsman. He loved baseball. It was his life. His dream was to be a professional baseball player. And the daughter was...Well, the daughter was a mouse."

I looked up at her and laughed.

"A mouse? The daughter was an actual mouse?"

"Yes," Theresa said. "She was a mouse. She was quiet and saw things, but never said anything. She stayed hidden, did as she was told and stayed out of the way for the most part. She observed her surroundings. She became so skilled at staying silent and hidden that she could move about this house so that she was never stepped on by accident. She learned how to appear to be a good little mouse. And the family was happy with the way that they appeared because they believed in looking like they were living the All-American Dream."

"But?" I guessed, intrigued by her storytelling. Not even thinking for a moment that any of this was true.

"But, what?" she asked.

"There's got to be more to the story. I mean, no one even lives here anymore. This is a ghost house. What happened to them? Did they leave this house to live the All-American Dream somewhere else?"

"No," Theresa said as she turned her head away from me.

"Then, what?"

"The father became an alcoholic. The mother became neglectful. The brother went to a place far away, never to return. And the daughter, the mouse, became a *monster*."

"Oh," I sighed in disappointment.

Theresa looked at me again. She gave me a wicked looking smile, with her lips pressed together and vertical furrows between her brows. Then she said, "And they all lived happily ever after."

CHAPTER 5

Snap back to reality. My body was sore. I hadn't realized how late I had stayed out with Theresa until dawn threatened to break. I had finished the drawing of the ghost family's living room and Theresa confiscated it from me. She warned me that she should keep it and that I wasn't allowed to mention the drawing nor our visit to the abandoned home to anyone. When I had inquired as to why I wasn't allowed to mention the visit or the drawing, she answered me by punching me in my right arm. It was a good thing that I was mostly left-handed. Theresa seemed to have had an affinity for injuring my right side. It didn't occur to me to argue with her or fight back at that point in our relationship.

Driving in my mom's car with Theresa beside me, I felt my muscles betray me with pain. My head swam with dizziness and my eyeballs struggled to stay open. I hadn't had food or taken my insulin according to my regular schedule. I hadn't taken my antidepressants or anxiety medication since yesterday morning. I felt the heaviest of symptoms from my diabetes. That was what was most prevalent now, according to me, since every time I looked over at Theresa I felt relief from any depression. However, I knew that I was going to pass out if I didn't get some kind of food inside of me.

"Where do you live?" I asked as I drove out of the ghost family's neighborhood.

"Just go back to Ryan's house and drop me off there. I can walk." Theresa said.

"Just tell me where you live. I can find it. You don't have to walk. Besides, you're only wearing my shirt and shorts. That's not a lot of clothes."

"So, what?"

"So, what?" I asked. "It looks weird and you shouldn't walk around like that!"

"Who are you? My father? You can have the damn clothes, Daniel. I don't need them." She said as she began taking off my shorts.

I tried to drive, but her anger bothered me too much. I pulled over on the side of the road and put the car in park.

"Stop it, Theresa!"

Theresa didn't get my shorts off completely. She hopped out of the car and pulled the shorts back up over her waist. I jumped out of the car and stopped her before she could walk away.

"Please," I told her. "Please get back in the car. I'm not trying to tell you what to do. I just want to take you home. That's all."

My heart beat out of my chest. The stare that she gave me scared me, with her hair all wild and her eyes big, angry and piercing. She stared at me crazily.

Without another word, Theresa got back into the car. I waited until she shut the door and sat back in her seat before I got back into the car.

I started the car and pulled off. I wanted to say something to her, but she seemed upset. Afraid that I would anger her more, I drove her to Ryan's house as she had requested. I pulled up to Ryan's driveway and parked. His front yard looked like a party had taken place the night before. Empty cans, bottles and cigarette butts lay on the lawn along with abandoned, random articles of clothing. Ryan's front door stood wide open as if it was waiting for someone to come inside and burgle the home. I looked over at Theresa concerned.

"Are you sure this is where you want me to drop you off?"

"Get off of it, Danny!" Theresa yelled.

"What? I just want to make sure you're okay. I can take you home if you want. This is...it's just..."

"It's just what?" she asked.

I shook my head and turned away from her. She had a way of making me feel so small.

"Exactly," Theresa said as she opened the car door. "I'll see you at school on Monday. Thanks for the ride."

She got out of the car, slammed my passenger side door and ran towards Ryan's front door. I watched her, wanting to shout at her, but I stayed silent. Before she went inside the house, she didn't even look up at me. She shut the door and that was the last I had seen of Theresa that weekend.

I tried not to let the physical pain that I was feeling get to me and distract me as I drove home. But the emotional pain of mixed emotions seemed to drive me insane. I blasted the radio with loud, emotionally screaming music to drown out my thoughts of rage. I wanted to go back to Ryan's house, find Theresa and throw her into the car and *make her* take me to her house. I wanted to know where she really lived and what it looked like. I wanted into her world. But that was not how it worked. I couldn't do that. So, I drove home. And as the sun began to rise, I felt my head grow fuzzy with the light of day as it broke through my windshield and reminded me that it was only Saturday and that Mom would be pissed at me when I got home.

I had told her that I was going to get a pack of cigarettes. I hadn't brought my cell phone with me. It was just a matter of time before I arrived at home and my mom would show how disappointed she was at me and how worried she had been. Perhaps I can use my diabetes as an excuse. I thought. I never tried it before. Never had to. Then again, I hadn't ever done anything like stay out all night with a girl before.

When I arrived home, I parked at the end of the driveway. It took a moment for me to get out of the car. I sat in the driver's seat trying to make sense of the night before and what had transpired between Theresa and me that morning as we parted ways. I looked over at Tom's house. It was quiet. His car was parked in his driveway like it hadn't moved at all the night before. I felt a bit of relief because I knew that if my mom had been really worried, she would have sent Tom out to find me and if that hadn't worked, she would have had Tom gather a search party. It didn't seem like it had gone to that extreme. I dragged myself out of my mom's car and slowly paced myself towards the house.

The clouds hung low. The hum of suburban silence and vehicles creeping into driveways on a Saturday morning rang in the air. My world was gray. And my head, cloudy. I stuck my house key into the lock with dread. Imagining that my mom had more soda cans to throw at my head. I envisioned that as soon as I revealed myself and shown her that I had not returned with cigarettes, she'd attack me with cans full of cola and citrus flavors. They're her favorite.

The door opened and I peered in, risking my head being pummelled. Silence and the smell of stale cigarettes and cold air greeted me. Why the hell was it so cold when it was so close to summer? I thought to myself. It wasn't cold outside. It was cold inside as if no one had lived here. It reminded me of the house with the religious family who had a daughter-mouse who became a monster and they lived happily ever after.

Slightly worried, I walked in and called out to my mom. She didn't answer. She wasn't at work. She didn't work on weekends. I looked over at the sofa where she had been sitting when we last spoke. She wasn't there. My vision was blurry, but I could tell that no one was here. I checked her bedroom, my bedroom, the kitchen, the bathroom that we both shared and the laundry room/pantry. She was not there!

I began to feel my heart beat fast. I started practicing my breathing the way that my doctor had taught me. Count one, two, three and start over again with each breath that I take. I did that as I stepped out the front door. My chest wanted to cave in as I breathed harder, faster.

I have the car, I thought to myself. Where could she have gone? I turned to Tom's house. His car was in the driveway. Dizziness made me weary, but I stepped down from the porch anyway. I stumbled. Of course, I fell to my knees. I hadn't eaten since yesterday, Friday, lunchtime at school when Theresa approached me and asked me for a cigarette. Sure, I had given her one the day before and the day before that. In fact, I remembered, as I scrambled to my feet and began struggling to Tom's house next door, that I had smoked three cigarettes each day before Theresa had asked me if she could have one.

I couldn't see the numbers on Tom's door. The doorbell looked as if a cloud had taken over the knobby, white buzzer. I pressed what had looked like a button. It made a ring-a-ding-like noise that played a vintage "midi" version of *Fur Elise* by Beethoven. I don't know why this made me laugh, but I found myself almost falling on my ass over it as it sadly played the classic melody.

No one answered, so I pressed the button again. The melody of strange chords played again. This time, I did not laugh. A familiar pain shot up my abdomen and back down my stomach and to my kidneys. I needed food, but I was standing at Tom's front door searching for something. My mind became muddy and I couldn't remember why I was there. When no one answered, I looked at his driveway again. His vehicle was parked. Perhaps he was asleep.

Sleep sounded good to me. I stumbled back to my house. I didn't realize that I had left the door wide open. I walked inside and made sure to shut the door behind me and lock it.

"Mom!" I called out to her.

She didn't answer.

I walked towards the kitchen and saw my blood sugar meter sitting on the kitchen table. Immediately, I pressed the button on the meter to turn it on. I couldn't find my tools to prick my finger. So, I bit down into my index finger until it bled. Then I let the blood drip onto the meter. I felt dizzy, cold, hot and anxious. I needed a shower, but I couldn't even see the refrigerator clearly enough to find the eggs to cook an omelet.

The meter screamed at me, "fifty five!"

"MOOOOOOOOOM!" I shouted as loud as I could.

Still, she did not answer me.

My body ached. My vision was blurry. My head felt dizzy, fuzzy and light. My blood sugar was low and dropping as I stumbled towards the refrigerator.

I found a leftover, chocolate birthday cake inside that Tom had brought over for mom a couple of days before on her 45th birthday. I tried to call out to her once more, but the effort was futile.

The cake tasted wonderful as I stuffed my face with it using my bare hands. I didn't bother to cut it. I didn't care to size up or manage portions like I had been taught to do by my primary care doctor. I simply dug into it and ate until it was finished.

I sat on the floor with the fudge icing on my hands and fingers. I licked them as best as I could before I crawled towards my bedroom. My stomach ached and my headache grew worse.

"Ugggggghhh," I cried as I pushed my bedroom door open from the floor.

The smell of stale sheets and dried bleach overwhelmed my nostrils. It looked like my mom and Tom did their best to clean my room. My bed sheets were changed. My wastebasket that had old cigarette butts and my favorite cartoon character shorts was emptied. Mine and Theresa's clothes and shoes that I had tossed in the washing machine had been washed, dried and dumped onto my bed. I made my way to the bed, and, with all of my little strength, pushed that stuff off of my bed and climbed onto it to let myself free of my clothes. I stripped down to nothing and just lay there on the bed, trying to breathe and grab a hold of my mind before it escaped me.

My bedroom grew dark, or was it my mind?

Mom didn't answer her phone. Nor was Tom answering his phone. I checked my voice mail on my cell, but the only message was from my best friend, E.J. I didn't feel like calling him back. From his garbled voice message, it seemed like he knew about Theresa and me. He knew that we had left school together on Friday. His message was almost incomprehensible with all of his excited shouting and sarcastic shrieks of wonder. I didn't have time for it. I couldn't even keep my eyes open. I dropped my phone and closed my eyes. Lying on my bed, I drifted off into a Saturday lovesick, diabetic sugar high. I went from low to high physically and emotionally. But I was way too weak to do anything about my emotional high. Unfortunately, the high blood sugar made me pass out on my bed while, emotionally, I wanted to run and shout out to Theresa around her neighborhood until I could find her house. My body wasn't going to allow it. So, my mind ran away from me as I drifted off into sleep.

Somehow, I did level out right before Monday, when it was time for me to go back to school. I didn't know how it happened and if anyone had helped me since I had passed out on that Saturday morning. I didn't wake up until my mom stormed into my room on Monday morning ten minutes before I had to leave for school.

The top of my left arm ached. Dried blood caked around my index finger where I had bitten myself. My blood glucose meter sat beside my bed on my nightstand and an empty syringe lay beside it. Was it Mom or Tom? Either way, I was grateful. I didn't say anything about the cake and her absence when I needed her on Saturday. Perhaps she was too upset and we were too rushed for her to bring it up.

"You are going to be late!" My mom shouted as she stormed into my bedroom on Monday morning.

I blinked my eyes slowly.

"Get up!" she screamed. Her shrillness made me want to curl up under my bed sheets. She must've sensed it because she ripped the sheets from over me and revealed my nakedness. She was unmoved.

"Mom..." I tried to yell, but only a whisper came out.

"Daniel, I'm not in a good mood right now. You have to get up and take your medicine and get ready to go to school. If you don't hurry, you'll miss the bus and we'll have to get Tom to take you to school. He's done enough already. I don't want to wake him up this early again."

I was so damn confused. The dizziness had passed. I didn't feel hungry and I didn't feel like I had eaten the sugar from Mom's birthday cake that surely would have killed me without me taking my insulin. I had eaten the whole cake!

"Mom, what are you doing? It's Sunday," I said.

"No! It's not Sunday. Daniel, it's Monday! You've slept all weekend and now it's time to get your ass up and get ready for school."

"What?"

"Get up!" My mom shouted as she threw some clothes at me.

Without caring, I put on the pair of blue jeans and the t-shirt with the Adventure Time characters printed on the front. She left my room before I could say or ask anything. I figured she was mad at me.

I went to the bathroom and emptied my bladder. Then with aching muscles, I continued to dress myself.

When I was fully dressed, I took my meds and tested my blood sugar. It was a good level at 110. Then I left the house without saying anything to my mom. She was mad at me, but I hadn't done anything to her all weekend, except borrow her car and maybe cause her to worry. That was nothing. She had been through worse. At least I came back instead of ending up in jail like my Pop.

I grabbed my hoodie, backpack and my cell phone. Then I headed out the door. As soon as I started walking towards the school bus stop, E.J. called me. I let the phone ring so that it would send him to voice mail. I had learned to stop pressing the red button to reject a phone call after my mom told me that she knew when I was ignoring her calls. I wondered how she knew what I had been doing. She said that when I pressed the red button while it was ringing it made her hear a beep sound and then the rings were cut short. After that, she'd hear the voice mail prompt. When that happened, it meant, on the other end, I saw that she called and had rejected her call.

I didn't want E.J. to think that I was avoiding him. I knew that I'd catch up with him at school. I was sure that he had many questions about what had happened and why I had left school early on Friday, let alone with Theresa. I'm sure he was wondering why I had not answered my phone all weekend. I was nervous about going into school that morning. Especially, since I had so many things happen in the last 72 hours, but I had very little answers as to how or why.

CHAPTER 6

Eduardo Jorge is my best friend. I call him E.J. because it's easier and because that's what everyone else calls him. Except, his mom, Xiomara Jorge. She calls him something else that I can't really pronounce. Moreover, I often get the overwhelming urge to want to call him Edward George because it's funny and it annoys the hell out of him.

E.J. is Hispanic. You can tell by his name, *Eduardo*. However, you can't really see it when you look at him. E.J. has brown skin, and soft, black hair. He's tall. He's so tall that he looks like he could play for the *Bulls*. We often played basketball together. He was good. However, E.J. described himself as "a lover, not a fighter". He was a non-competitive kind of guy who watched sports and other games from the sidelines when it came to real competition. We'd go out to the park and play basketball together for exercise, but art is our favorite thing to do together.

E.J. sticks beside me in art class and chooses to mix his various oil paints together in hopes of becoming the next Michelangelo or Dali. I stick with my canvas paper, charcoal pencils and lead pencils in hopes of being able to draw something that looks great, but doesn't become too personal to the point where I don't want to look at it.

E.J. speaks English fluently, but his first language is Spanish. His family is from Panama. E.J. was born here in Georgia, USA. He's the first generation in his family to go to school in America, along with his little sister, Rozella.

I've met his family. They invited me over for festive dinners and celebrations. I went to his sister's sweet 16 birthday party. Rozella was given $2500 and a five-foot sweet butter-cream cake in the shape of her favorite Disney Princess.

His family is wonderful and intimidating in many ways. They all have brown skin of various shades and eyes that range from the darkest, chestnut browns to the brightest greens and blues that contrast with their beautiful skin tones. On top of their almost mystifying physical beauty, they are the most passionately caring people that I know. They're a close, tight-knit family. They support everything that E.J. does including his creative and artistic passions. And at his sister's birthday party, they spent an unmentionable amount of money on a singing group that his sister was a fan of so that she would have a night to remember.

When I asked E.J. why they would spend so much money on only one night, E.J. simply said, "Because we love Rozy." Then he looked at me as if I should understand what he was talking about without any further explanation. As if to say that *love is enough*.

The Jorges greet each other with kisses on both cheeks, long hugs that require squeezing and a slight sniff of each other's necks. It's almost as if they want you to be aware of the fact that they are touching you. It's not something you're ever going to be able to run away from nor need to be ashamed.

While I do appreciate that his family has that kind of bond, I was glad that E.J. didn't greet me like that when we saw each other.

"Dan! Aww man," E.J. said as we walked towards each other outside of the school.

We saw each other as soon as we got off our school buses. He was dressed in the latest highfalutin fashions of the nearing summer. His clothes looked clean, carefully tailored and pressed. I looked like I had just rolled out of bed and thrown on the only clean jeans and cheap cartoon t-shirt that was available to me.

E.J. was dressed in a neatly pressed, light blue knitted, collared shirt and ironed khaki shorts. His hair was styled and combed up in a curly Afro, neatly upon his head. My hair was wild, ethnically accurate to my mixed, Northern Irish-Black American heritage: black, curly at the edges, straight at the roots, and tangled with hints of nappy in between. My hair looked like it had not been brushed, combed or washed since the week before. I hadn't had time for a haircut, nor did I bother to make time for one. My hair chaotically hung over my eyes and draped down the back of my neck.

"You look like she put you through hell, man," E.J. laughed as we grabbed each other's right hand, locked fingertips and brought each other in for a light chest bump. E.J. patted my back with his left hand. I heard him sniff my neck. This made me feel a bit awkward, but I knew it was what he was used to. I let it go without argument.

"So, Dan!" E.J. laughed.

"So?" I said as we began to walk into school.

"You left school early on Friday. What happened to you?"

He teased me with a knowing grin on his face.

We stopped at our lockers that were next to each other. I opened my locker and started grabbing my first and second period books.

"I wasn't feeling well," I lied.

"And did Theresa make you feel better?"

I put my head into my locker and tried to close the door on my neck. E.J. laughed and grabbed the door so that I couldn't shut it on myself.

"Help me out, Dan! This is serious."

"No," I half whined and half laughed.

"Let me recall last Friday for you and you can pick up where I leave off. So, you and I were at lunch. One minute you told me you're going to the counter to get a bottle of water. The next minute I saw you talking to Theresa McElheney. Mind you, man, this is the fourth time that I saw you both talking to each other and standing close to each other last week. I turned away for one second to give Rozy some money for her ice cream and when I looked back up at you, you were gone. In one second! What happened?"

I closed my locker and tried to walk away from him, but E.J. was not going to leave me alone. I shook my head and tried to pick up my pace to head to my homeroom.

"Okay," E.J. said. "I get it. You don't want to kiss and tell. Just tell me one thing."

I stopped in front of my homeroom and turned to E.J. to indulge him.

"Did you finally hit it?"

"Really?" I laughed. "Hit it? Are you asking me if I hit Theresa? Hit her where? In her face? Are you serious?"

We laughed together. The warning bell rang for homeroom. E.J. started backing away and pointed at me.

"You're going to tell me," E.J. warned me.

"Yeah, okay," I laughed. "There's nothing to tell."

"I'm serious," E.J. said before he turned the corner at the end of the hallway and disappeared.

Kids began to scatter and run to try to make it to their homerooms before the tardy bell rang. I took my time standing in the hallway outside of Mr. Blankenship's classroom. I continued to laugh at E.J. long after he was gone. He was going to be a pain until I told him what had happened. It was funny to see him get so anxious about knowing everything. That was like him, though. If he cared about you, he had to know what you were doing and somehow had to be involved. I was glad that we didn't have homeroom together and that we wouldn't see each other until later because I would need the first part of the day to find Theresa. I needed to see her.

"What the hell are you laughing at, stupid?" someone said as they shoved me out of the way to get into Mr. Blankenship's classroom.

I looked up and saw that it was Rex King. Rex King and his herd of followers pushed past me. They elbowed and shoved me as they entered the classroom. These guys were big, so it was hard to get past them. Dressed in their blue and gold soccer team jackets and blue jeans, they all looked like they belonged to some clone-making Stepford society there at Cobb High School. They reeked of school spirit from head to toe. That's because Rex's soccer team was number one in the state. Automatically, it meant that they owned the school.

It seemed like Rex and his soccer teammates had all of the same classes together, including our homeroom. It was as if being out in the field and in the locker rooms together wasn't enough for them. They had to be together all of the time. Rex was so tough, or at least he thought he was while his minions surrounded him.

I glared at Rex as I walked past him in the classroom. He didn't say anything to me. He just stared back and grinned. I walked to the back of the classroom and sat down in my assigned seat. Mr. Blankenship told everyone to settle down as he did a roll call. Then the tardy bell rang.

It would be so nice to see what Rex would be like without those guys around him. I wondered how mighty he would be and if he'd have the audacity to shove me again. The thought of what could happen if I had a chance to face him alone made me smile all through homeroom period. I imagined lots of flying fists and blood and perhaps getting my hands on that blue and gold jacket and burning that shit to ashes.

CHAPTER 7

Trying to avoid E.J. was like trying to avoid going to the bathroom. After a while, it catches up with you and you just have to deal with it. E.J. and I were in the same art class. I knew that I was going to run into him eventually.

As I walked towards the art building of our school, I saw E.J. standing outside talking to someone. At first, I couldn't see this person's face completely because I was still coming from around the other side of the building. The person was dressed like a fashion show was going on somewhere. Therefore, I assumed E.J. was talking to another art student. However, when I came around the corner of the building and started getting closer to them, I was able to get a clearer view of this guy's face. I realized it was Ryan.

It was shocking at first to see the two of them talking to each other. What does Ryan have to say to E.J.? And why would E.J. even entertain the company of someone like Ryan? It didn't make sense to me. The more I thought about it, the angrier it made me. I almost walked away until I heard my name come out of Ryan's mouth.

E.J. stood on the side of the art building with his

backpack thrown over his left shoulder. He listened intently to Ryan. Ryan didn't have any books in his hands. He didn't have art classes with us. He stood there face to face with E.J. He looked serious and sounded upset as he spoke.

"Listen! Tell your friend, Daniel to stay the hell away from my house. He's not welcome," Ryan said.

I backed up when I heard my name and moved back around the corner so that they wouldn't see me, but I stayed close enough to be able to hear their conversation.

"Daniel was at your house? When?" E.J. asked. He seemed shocked.

"He came to my house on Friday night and crashed my party," Ryan tattled.

E.J. seemed to have to adjust himself before replying. He paused and took a step back.

"So, what's your problem with him, Ryan?" E.J. asked.

"My problem is that your boy, Daniel, don't know how to relax. The only things that we do are party and get laid. Nothing else. I don't have time for people who take life too seriously or who has any other agenda. They don't get my time or energy. And that bitch boy, Daniel, is one of them. He came to my party on Friday looking for a fight. Nobody fights at my parties. But here comes his stupid ass looking for Theresa. Grabbing her up and taking her away when he saw that she was having a good time! Man, if I wasn't already high, I would've kicked his ass out myself. It's a good thing for him that he and Theresa left before it went there."

E.J. shook his head, seeming as if he had to take it all in at once. Well, this was the first time he had heard about what had happened on Friday night. It was the first time I had ever done anything like that before. I'm sure it was a shock to him. After all, I did deny him of the chance to hear it straight from me and in a more pleasant tone. My point of view would have provided a better explanation. He should have heard it from me, his best friend. Instead, he had to hear it from a piss-ant.

"Well umm," E.J. coughed out, "I'll talk to Daniel."

"Fine," Ryan said with a hard and clear sigh. "He's a psycho. I don't understand how you're his friend."

"That's not your problem to worry about," E.J. said as he walked away from Ryan.

I felt my head begin to swell with anger. Spots of red began to cloud my vision and I found myself starting to walk towards Ryan. Fortunately, E.J. saw me appear from around the corner of the building and he approached me before I could get near Ryan.

"Dan," E.J. said, "Class is this way. Where are you going? Come on, we're going to be late."

At that moment, the warning bell rang. The spots of red began to dissipate from my eyesight. Ryan had turned his back on us when he saw me come around the corner. Immediately, Ryan ran towards the main school building. He was far out of my reach by the time E.J. caught up with me. The sound of the warning bell seemed to have woken me up.

"Yeah, right," I said as I watched Ryan disappear into the main school building.

I was disappointed because I didn't get a chance to say hello to Ryan. Perhaps he would have had the audacity to tell me how he really felt straight to my face. Instead of going to my best friend and telling on me like a damn coward.

"You alright?" E.J. asked as we walked into the classroom.

"Yeah," I sighed.

As we entered the art room, the scent of fresh wet paint on new canvases, Georgia clay and porcelain that had just been fired in the kiln filled the room. Our teacher, Mrs. Greer, continued to present sculptures that she seemed to have favored from her students. The tardy bell rang, and more students continued to pour into the classroom. Mrs. Greer didn't seem to care that quite a few of them were late. She smiled happily and wiped her hands on her apron.

"Come in! Guys and gals this is an exciting day!" Mrs. Greer exclaimed.

Her excitement made the whole class overwhelmed with joyful curiosity and fervor. I looked at E.J. and he shrugged his shoulders and smiled.

"We have the final round of the State's Art Competition coming up! As I told you before, only one person from each category will be chosen to face off with our rivals in other counties. We are the only ones in our region to actually have a student qualify for each category in the competition!"

My colleagues cheered and clapped their hands while eagerly awaiting Mrs. Greer's announcement of the names of the students who made it to the final round.

I stared out of the window, hoping to see Theresa and wanting a cigarette, badly. I didn't hear the names she called starting with who placed first for clay sculpting. Followed by the best mixed medium artist in the class. Then she called out the name of some kid who made something he called art out of spoons, knives and other eating utensils that he glued to a blank lambskin canvas.

People loved that shit. I didn't understand it, but to each his own. Best painter award went to someone other than E.J. He seemed disappointed not to hear his name called. He stood beside his oil painting of a man playing a trombone. The man in the painting looked happy as he sat alone outside of a villa underneath the hot sun in some village that I'm sure E.J. had created from his own imagination. I couldn't fathom how he lost first place to a kid who painted dots and swirls in a chaos of yellows, blues, pinks and greens on a black background. It didn't make any sense. It looked like one of those paintings that people waste millions of dollars on that are painted by elephants and monkeys.

When this kid was asked to explain what their art was about they simply said, "It's about life."

What the...?

I turned to E.J. He sat on a stool, looking down at his hands. His painting of the lonely trombone player sat on the easel beside him. He looked defeated. He wouldn't even look at it. He just stared at his hands.

As Mrs. Greer went down her list of top artists who will go on to the State Art Competition, I tried to block out her voice. I didn't want to hear anymore about the garbage, a cop-out art piece that "is about life". What a load of crap!

"And finally, for charcoal and lead category, Mr. Daniel Buachailluathúil Blackwell." Mrs. Greer proudly announced.

I looked up, confused, shocked and... did she *really* just say my whole name?

"What?" I asked.

"Daniel, you made it to the State Art Competition. Your charcoal and lead drawing of the Midtown

Memorial is a winner. Congratulations!" Mrs. Greer spoke as if she was inviting me to some special party where I was supposed to be as excited as she was to be attending.

I remained confused. People were staring at me. No one cheered or clapped like they did for the others. In fact, the room was completely silent. Even E.J. sat there on his stool, staring at me as if I was supposed to say something.

"Well," Mrs. Greer said with a heavy sigh. "I am one very proud teacher to have students from my class, at our school, take a place in every art category for the State Art Competition. I think that we should all celebrate today. Feel free to grab a canvas. Grab some clay. Grab your paints and pencils. Grab any sword of your choice and go into the battle of creativity. Feel free to step outside of your preferred medium. Be daring! Go against the rules! Go against the man! Express yourselves freely today."

Some guy named Kenny Valleywood stood in front of the class and started to take his clothes off as everyone cheered and laughed in joy and celebration. I looked back outside of the window, not sure if I was still inside of my own body. The world felt surreal. My mind began to race towards Theresa and how many cigarettes I could smoke to get her to come to me.

"I said be free. However, don't take your clothes off. We are not drawing or sculpting anything with nudity. Kenny, put your shirt back on. I know that I said to go against the man, but there are still laws that we must abide by here in school. Perhaps when you're in college you can get away with that. For now, you can express yourself, but you have to keep your clothes on!

Now, go on. Be free! Live and love through your art!"
Mrs. Greer exclaimed. She threw her hands into the air,
raised her arms above her head and gave two claps, and
made a sort of "cuck-coo" bird chirping sound as if that
was her battle cry for her soldiers to go to war.

A cigarette. I wanted a damn cigarette! I folded my
arms against the windowpane and stared out at the open
field behind the art building. The soccer field stared back
at me mockingly. The window was wide open. A warm
breeze blew in and hit me in the face. Summer was
coming, and I was anticipating the freedom from athletes
and overly excited and condescending teachers who
called you by your first, middle and last name in front of
everyone in your class. They had no idea what the hell it
all means. I didn't even know what it meant. And the fact
that she said it perfectly, just like how my mom used to
say it when I was a little kid freaked me out even more.
Whenever Mom was angry with me, she'd call me by my
full name. I never really learned how to pronounce it
right. It was Irish, or Gaelic, or something. I didn't know
at the time.

Upset, I spat out the window a huge glob of
phlegm that was lodged somewhere between my uvula
and nasal passage.

"Mr. Blackwell?" I heard Mrs. Greer bellow out in
a singsong kind of way from way too close behind me.

I turned around and she was practically so close to
my face, I could smell her caramel latte breath and see
the coffee stains on her teeth as she smiled widely. She
spoke through her teeth, patiently.

"You made it to the State Art Competition. You
get to represent Cobb High this year in your chosen art
medium. This could lead to great opportunities for you in

the future."

"Really?" I tried to sound interested.

"Yes," she said. "You could network with other artists. Colleges and Universities are always at these competitions looking to give out scholarships to students who show great passion and promise."

I put my feet up on the windowpane as I sat there and began to fumble with my shoelaces. Where the hell is Theresa? I thought to myself. I need a cigarette. Perhaps if I had three cigarettes to smoke, then she'd come to me like she did before. The magic number is three. That's it! Three! I have to find three cigarettes.

"Daniel?" Mrs. Greer called out me with sort of a whimper in her voice.

I turned back to her, blinked and shook my head.

"No thanks," I said.

E.J. came out of nowhere and put his hand over my mouth.

"Umm Mrs. Greer, what he means to say is he'd like to think it over and he'll get back to you," E.J. said, trying to save me somehow. "He just needs to look at all of the rules and figure out what he wants to present. You know how it goes with competitions. You have to read the fine print and everything before you sign on the dotted line. So, umm, yeah, Daniel is definitely interested. He needs time to figure out what he's going to do. So, yes, please he wants to be a part of this competition."

Mrs. Greer looked concerned. E.J.'s hand remained over my mouth as I didn't struggle or try to say anything. I guess he kept it there just in case I tried to say something stupid.

"Is that right, Mr. Blackwell?" Mrs. Greer asked.

"Do you want to accept your place in the competition?"

I started to shake my head no, but E.J.'s hand slid from my mouth and gripped my jaw and he made me nod my head yes.

"Wonderful!" Mrs. Greer cheered. "This is a great opportunity for you, Mr. Blackwell. After all, your drawing was the most impressive out of all of the pieces that were considered. You should feel proud. I'm honored as your teacher. Now, people, get to work. Today, I want you to reach deep within yourselves. Make something that expresses you and today."

Whatever the fuck that means, I thought to myself as E.J. released me from his grip.

Mrs. Greer walked away and went on to pester the sculptors. Everyone else seemed happy and proud of their accomplishments. I just wanted a cigarette and to talk to Theresa. I didn't even know that I had been entered into a competition. I didn't remember signing up for it. However, I wasn't shocked to hear my name called as a finalist for the State Art Competition.

E.J. looked disappointed, but when he looked at me, he seemed to be happy for me. He smiled, put his hand on my shoulder and gave it a squeeze.

"Congratulations, Dan," E.J. said with sincerity in his voice.

"Thank you?" I asked him.

"I guess," he answered. "I mean, aren't you happy?"

I shrugged and got up from the windowsill. I grabbed a drawing pad from a pile of canvases in the front of the room. I picked up a box of charcoal pencils, sat at my easel and blanked out.

E.J. had already begun painting with a big brush.

He dipped the tip of the brush into a glob of yellow paint and began to spread it onto a square, white linen canvas. His hands moved easily with the brush at his tips. The yellow turned into a corner of a sky, making circles. Then he used other brushes of various sizes to outline his sky with different shades of blue, purple and gray. His sky looked bruised, but bandaged with that corner of yellow, like the sun after a rainy day.

My drawing pad remained blank. I continued to watch E.J. Then he punctured his serene sky with a big blob of paint. It made a black dot in the middle of his serene sky. Suddenly, the painting turned into something that reminded me of the world ending.

I looked away, moved by what I saw. Frightened. Afraid that I'd never see Theresa again and there would be no more cigarettes to smoke because the black dot swallowed it up in E.J.'s sky and it lied to me.

"Are you stuck?" E.J. asked.

"No, I just...I don't know. I need to smoke," I admitted.

"Yeah, well, you're going to get a zero for the day if you don't draw something. Not smoking will be the least of your problems. Come on, you're still on academic probation. Don't mess this up, Dan. Draw something. Anything. Draw me!"

I froze up.

"No! No, E.J. I can't draw you," I said as I picked at my shoelaces.

"Why not?" E.J. asked. "It's easy. It's a free pass day. If you can't think of what to draw, you can just draw me. It's an easy, passing grade."

"No it's not!" I yelled at him. Anger built up inside of me. Earlier that day, I saw him talking to Ryan about me. I heard what they had said and he hadn't even brought it up to me yet. "You don't understand! I can't just draw you! It's not like that!" I didn't want to see him through my eyes in that vulnerable way.

Everyone in the room seemed to look at me all at the same time. Mrs. Greer gestured to me to see if I was all right. I took a deep breath and nodded at her.

"I'm sorry," I said to E.J. as I tried to calm myself down. "I mean, I just want to draw the outside. I'm good with buildings and landscapes anyway. Thanks, though."

E.J. nodded and silently went back to his painting. I wasn't sure if he was mad at me for yelling at him or not. Knowing E.J., he probably chose to let it go. That was like him. He didn't hang on to petty things. He was mellow and low key, but he wasn't a push over. That kind of balance was something I wish I had. It was something I wish that I could understand how to handle and control. But it wasn't that easy for me.

I drew the soccer field with the goals, the bleachers, the flowers and trees. I drew it all with the anger and rage that I felt inside of me. I waited for E.J. to tell me about his conversation with Ryan. I waited for him to ask me again about last Friday and what had happened with Theresa. But he didn't say anything. He wouldn't tell me about his painted black dot that ruined the sky. Quietly, he finished his assignment and cleaned up when he was finished.

I looked over at his painting. The sky was normal. The sun still caressed the transition in the sky from day into night with its various colors of blues, purples and grays. It turned out, that black dot was not a black dot at all. It was an airplane rising into the sky and taking off somewhere towards the sunset. The painted world below was so small. Much like real life.

My drawing was messy. It was shallow and full of resentment. Smudges of charcoal pretended to be shadows and crooked lines of the soccer field. Shapes and figures of make believe people acted as if they cared about being on my canvas of a make believe happy life. They were inside of my dumb world of insulin and anti-depressants from when I was diagnosed with Juvenile Diabetes at thirteen years old. I was diagnosed just in time for varsity soccer try-outs. The drawing, smeared with the charcoal mess of a mother of a sick boy. Between the lines, you can see that she's more emotional and scared than he is. So, she keeps him from doing anything like playing sports. And the askew drawing of the grass, flowers and trees represented a father who was just not there at the time because he was held up somewhere where he couldn't be let out until a judge of some county court said that he could be free.

I don't care about sports, I thought to myself. I didn't want to get past JV soccer anyway. I am an artist, I told myself. Besides, I am not a blue and gold clone. They want me to compete for the State Art Competition. Isn't that still representing the blue and gold?

As E.J. stood at the sink washing off his paint brushes, I took two of his bottles of paint from the desk that was propped up beside his easel. I picked up blue and brown paint. Brown was the closest to gold that I could find in E.J.'s collection of paints. I unscrewed the top of the bottles where if you squeeze it, the paint would shoot out like liquid silly string. I aimed the paint at my drawing and squeezed the bottles. I waved my arms and twisted my wrists until it began to hurt my hands. The blue and brown paint brought color to my world of black charcoal and lead.

When I stopped, I noticed that I had paint all over my hands and some of it had dripped onto the floor. I looked at my piece of artwork. The charcoal soccer field looked as if it was bleeding with the spirit of the blue and gold ringers. As if they had all been slaughtered out there on the field and all that was left were the crushed dreams of those who could and would have been.

Mrs. Greer walked up and stood beside me. She stared at my marvelous mess and gasped. She put her hands to her lower neck as if she was grabbing at something invisible.

She asked, "Daniel, what do you call this?"

As my Pop used to say to me in a stone-wall kind of tone, I replied to her in a weird replica of his voice, "Shoulda! Coulda! Woulda!"

CHAPTER 8

At lunchtime, I was able to bum a cigarette off Christian. A guy who didn't live up to his name by choice. He sold everything from cigarettes to plants and pills that would take any eager buyer to another so called dimension. I didn't test those grounds. I had enough surreal, freaky madness surrounding me.

Christian let me have a cigarette in exchange for a drawing that I did of a girl that he liked. That girl turned out to be McKayla. McKayla was easy to draw. She was easy to read. She was the girl who represented school spirit, blue and gold. She was doted on because she was Dr. Flemming's daughter and a brilliant straight A student.

Like Christian, she was into drugs and psychedelic concoctions of her own making. Surely, this girl was going to be our classes' valedictorian at our graduation next year. If only they knew how smart she really was. McKayla was the dangerous kind of intelligent that would get somebody killed. Because she had popular charm that she presented through smoke and mirrors and her potent inventions, she was able to get away with anything. Even murder.

Why did Christian care so much about her? I didn't

know. At the time, I didn't even care. I gave him the sketch that I did of her in biology class and he handed me a stale loosie.

"Hey," I said. "You think that I can get two more?"

Christian laughed and shook his head.

"Come on, Christian," I pleaded.

Christian looked down at the lead pencil sketch of his freaky darling crush and laughed. He reached into his pocket and pulled out a pack of Newport's. I threw my head back and sighed, rolling my eyes. I hate Newport's, but whatever.

Christian pulled out two more loosies and held them out to me. As I reached out for them, he pulled them back and said, "Talk to her for me."

I raised my eyebrows and widened my eyes.

"I'm serious," Christian said. "You can talk to her for me. Tell her to holler at me. That's all you have to do."

Baffled, I said, "I don't know why you want me to talk to McKayla for you. She's not really approachable."

"And that's why you're going to do it for me," Christian said.

"What the heck do you want me to say?"

"Just go up to her and tell her that 'Christian wants to holler at you'. I don't know. I heard you were at Ryan's party. When I tried to go, Ryan kicked me out. I didn't even get past the driveway. McKayla's always there at Ryan's house. I heard you left with Theresa McElheney. If you can leave with her, then you must be in. Right? So, when you go back, just talk to McKayla for me."

Who else knew about this? My face burned. My cheeks stung. Sweat began to build up and dribble down from my temples. I ran my hand over my face and nodded to Christian as if I had damn clue. There was just one problem. Ryan didn't want me back at his house. It probably didn't matter if McKayla or Theresa was there, Ryan didn't want me to go to his house.

"Yeah, okay," I said. I could hear my voice trembling. "Sure. I'll tell McKayla to call you."

Christian held the cigarettes out to me again. I took them from him.

"That's what I'm talking about. Let's exchange phone numbers," he said as he pulled out his cellular phone. "Give me your number and I'll send you text so that you'll know it's me."

Reluctantly, I gave Christian my mobile number. I watched him as he eagerly punched the numbers into his phone, grinning and cunningly it seemed.

"You're in," he said with a smile.

Not smiling, I said, "Great..."

"Don't let me down, Daniel." Christian said.

Nodding to him, I walked away with the three cigarettes, filled with hope. I didn't hear the last of what he had said. He shouted something about tapping something of McKayla's with a thing that I didn't want to know. He was a strange person. I realized that he worried me just as much as McKayla weirded me out.

I stepped outside at lunchtime and began to suck down the first cigarette. The first drag was so long that I made myself choke and cough.

"You should quit that mess," a serious and friendly voice stated from behind me.

I turned slightly to see E.J. coming down the stairs of the main building on the quad. He had four books in his hand and a thick backpack on his shoulders. He sat them down on the stairs and then squatted down beside me.

"Want some?" I joked as I blew smoke out away from his face.

E.J. gave me the same look that I once saw his mom give him when we were in middle school. He had told her that when he graduated high school, he was going to become a ringleader for a traveling Turkish circus.

I laughed and coughed at the memory.

"See," E.J. said. "That's why you need to quit smoking, Dan. Is that even good for you know your, um..."

"My what?" I asked him. I wanted him to say it.

"Your diabetes," E.J. said.

I was disappointed. I thought that he would have said something else. Everyone knew that I had diabetes. That was no big deal. People understood physical illnesses. They talked about it. They had walks and fundraisers to advocate for people with diabetes. But I felt like E.J. wanted to say something else.

"No," I said. "I'm fine."

"Okay."

There was a weird silence between us for about five minutes as I finished my first cigarette and began to light the second one. E.J. didn't say anything. He looked down at his books and fumbled with the pages. I started to laugh as I took my second puff. E.J. looked up at me and snickered, not knowing what I was laughing at. He smiled and let out a chuckle.

"What's funny?" E.J. asked.

"Earlier today, you!" I said.

"I just want to know about last Friday," E.J. said light heartedly.

"Didn't you already hear about it?" I said with some kind of resentment in my tone.

E.J. ignored it and continued to seem upbeat. "Kind of," he admitted. "But I had asked you what happened first. Are you going to tell me?"

I nodded, defeated. Wait. No, I was not defeated. I was inspired to tell E.J. because of Ryan's little pow-wow with him earlier. I didn't want E.J. to think that Ryan's story was the whole truth about what had happened. Then I began to tell him from the beginning about what had happened between Theresa and me from the moment we had left the lunchroom on Friday to the moment I saw him get off the school bus that morning.

"She asked me for a cigarette. It was the third one she had asked me for that day," I began. I told him how strange it was to have Theresa, of all girls, come on to me and follow me home.

"It was impulsive," I told E.J. "One minute we were walking to my house. The next moment, she was shoving me against the wall in my living room. Then suddenly, we were in my bedroom."

E.J. kept a calm face as I spoke of each and every detail about how Theresa aggressively seduced me. When I finally got to the part where I confessed that I was no longer a virgin, E.J. raised his eyebrows. His mouth made an excitedly shaped O and he let out a cheerful howl.

"Dan! My man," he exclaimed. "You did it!"

I lowered my head, blushing and trying not to make it seem like it was big deal.

"We did it again," I confessed. "That night, I picked her up from Ryan's party and we did it again."

E.J. laughed and threw his head back. He patted my back and gave me a gentle punch to my shoulder in approval.

"Finally," E.J. said. "My boy got some. But of all people! Theresa? I have to say, though, I'm not shocked."

"Why not?" I asked.

"She seemed to like you when we were in middle school. Think about all of those times she hit on you. She was bigger than you were back then, but she could only use that kind of aggressiveness to her advantage. It was messed up how she used to bully you. It's still kind of like that was the only way she could show you that she liked you."

I shook my head. Perhaps, he was right. E.J. would know better than I would since he'd had several girlfriends since middle school with which he'd had physical experiences. He would be able to understand better than I would at the time. But there was one thing here that he did not catch or even bring up. He missed where I had mentioned picking up Theresa from Ryan's house. That was his chance to talk to me. To tell me about the conversation he'd had with Ryan. E.J. didn't mention it as he continued to talk about the irony in my relationship with Theresa. He said that it didn't make sense, but somehow it did and there will be people who will think that it's a joke or not for real. He even suggested that our *relationship* seemed forced.

I listened to him, angrily. He didn't bring up his conversation with Ryan at all. When the lunch bell finally rang, I had already smoked all three cigarettes. I tossed the butt of the final cigarette into the grass.

"OK, I have to get to chemistry," I told E.J. "After all, I am on academic probation," I said, mockingly, the way that he had reminded me earlier. "I have to do everything that I can to not get kicked out of school."

E.J. must've caught my negative attitude, but he didn't provoke me any further.

"Yeah, sure," E.J. said. "I'll see you after school. We're still on for basketball at the park, right?"

"No," I said. "I have an appointment. I can't."

E.J. laughed. He said, "Oh yeah, I know what kind of appointment you have. Is Theresa going to be at that appointment? Give you some of that sexual healing?"

I nodded, lying and not caring. I turned my back on E.J. and walked away as he laughed on about protection. He made a joke that I didn't find to be very funny.

I did have an appointment, but it wasn't with Theresa. I had wished it were. It was with my doctor. It was time for a check up on my meds. But it wasn't the kind of doctor that helps me with my diabetes. It was the kind of doctor that helped me with depression, anxiety and manic episodes. The kind of doctor that I couldn't talk about with E.J. or Theresa. It was the kind of doctor that I felt a lot of shame when I thought about having to go to his office. You don't talk to your friends about this kind of doctor. You know, the psychiatrist.

CHAPTER 9

Theresa was not at school that day. I had overheard McKayla laughing about how hung over Theresa was, when she called her that morning to see if she wanted a ride to school. I had the urge to punch McKayla for some reason. I don't know why. She rubbed me the wrong way in every way. I wished that Theresa didn't hang out with her.

I waited for my mom to pick me up since I had a doctor's appointment. She had always picked me up from school on days I had to see the doctor. Instead, Tom's car pulled up to the kiss-and-ride parking lot.

"My mom told me not to get rides from strangers," I taunted him.

"Your mom sent me to pick you up," he said, ignoring my joke. "Get in."

Tom didn't seem to be in a good mood. Usually, he's pretty calm or upbeat and kiss ass like, but today he seemed serious and in a hurry.

I hopped into the front seat.

"Put on your seat belt," Tom demanded.

I tossed my books into the back seat and snapped the seat belt into place.

As soon as I had the seat belt on, Tom sped out of

the parking lot in a hot rage. He swerved and cut around cars so fast that it made the trees and everything else outside a blur. My heart rate sped up with each mile he sped up to faster. He went from 25 miles per hour to 65mph in under a minute.

"Slow down! Tom!" I shouted.

Tom didn't slow down. He didn't respond. He didn't even look at me.

"Come on, Tom! What the hell?" I cried, growing ever more afraid.

"What the hell? What the hell is with you, Daniel? Are you scared?" He asked, looking fiercely ahead of him at the road. He continued to weave in and out of traffic at a high speed.

"Yes! Why are you going so fast?" I asked.

Tom pulled onto the freeway and switched gears, causing him to go from 65 miles per hour to 75mph. He pushed his way onto the freeway from off of the ramp and cut off a car that was already on the freeway. The driver of that vehicle honked their horn at Tom and I could see them waving their fist at him angrily.

I shook my head in disbelief.

"Are you scared?" He asked again.

"Yes! Fuck! I'm scared! Why are you doing this?" I pulled at my hair and screamed.

"Good! Now, you know how it feels," he said in a much softer tone of voice, but sternly.

I looked at him and said, "Know how what feels?"

He didn't slow down. He sped up to 95 mph. Suddenly, I felt cramps in my stomach.

Tom said, "Do you know how your mother feels when she comes home to find you passed out and sick? Do you know how she feels when she has to clean up after you after one of your fits? Do you know how she feels when you go out all night and don't call? How do you think that makes her feel? She has enough to deal with as it is, as you're not taking care of yourself. When she found you on Saturday morning passed out, your blood sugar level was so high that she didn't know what to do. She couldn't wake you, no matter how hard she tried. You scared her! I had to give you a shot of insulin. You think that I like doing that?"

Tom had been driving so fast that I didn't realize he had already taken the ramp off the highway and was pulling into the parking lot of my psychiatrist's office.

"No," I said, embarrassed. I held back the vomit that I felt like I was going to spit up from my guts.

"It stops now, Daniel! All of it! I don't know if this has anything to do with that girl she found you with in your bedroom or if this is just some kind of teenage rebellion thing that you're testing out on your mom and me, but it is going to stop now!"

Thoughts started swarming in my head. I didn't like the way he was speaking to me, like he was my father or something. I didn't like the way he said *your mom and me*. What did that mean? Who the hell was he? He wasn't my father, stepfather, or my mother's boyfriend for that matter. And I especially didn't like the way he talked about Theresa. He didn't know anything.

Tom put the car in park and I took my seat belt off. I began to open the door, but Tom yanked me by the sleeve of my hoodie and stopped me. I looked down at his hand, wanting to break every bone in it. Then I raised my eyes up to him, keeping my head slightly down, giving him a look to warn him that he'd better let me go. I felt myself ready to go into a rage.

Tom may have sensed it. He let go and said, "It's not fair, kid. What you do to your mother. She only wants what's best for you. You have to look after yourself and not get into any trouble. Especially, now, at a time like this. She is...well...you have to be good. Be a good boy. Okay, Daniel?"

I turned away from him, not wanting to see the odd pain in his eyes. I didn't understand why it bothered him so much. I got out of the car and slammed the door.

"I'll be here when you get out," Tom yelled out the window to my back as it was turned to him.

I said as I walked away, "Don't worry about it. I'll take the bus or the train."

Without another word, I heard his car speed off. I turned around quickly to see if he had actually left me. He did. I stood on the pavement, waiting to see if he'd come back, but he didn't come back for me.

I hated sitting in the waiting room at Dr. Eren's office. There were all kinds of people there in different shapes, sizes, colors and ages. There was one thing in there that I wasn't sure what it was. It appeared to be a womanly like man but seemed more alien because she didn't have a real color to her. She was burly and short. She didn't have any kind of shades of brown, pink or beige to her skin. Her skin looked somewhat gray with hints of green. Her hair was dyed pink and green. Her skin wasn't wrinkled up like an old person's but she sat in a hunched over pose like an elderly person would sit. I tried not to stare at her, but she kept giving me strange glances, like she was trying to figure me out. Maybe I looked strange to her, too.

When my name was called, I felt relieved. Trade one waiting room for another. They put me in Dr. Eren's office and made me wait another 15 minutes before he finally walked in with my chart.

"How are you doing today, Daniel?" Dr. Eren asked as he shut the door. He kept his face down with his eyes buried in my chart, reading and no doubt trying to think of what to say next so that he can hurry up and get me out of his office. He never seemed to look at my face. We never made eye contact because he was always reading my chart, no doubt trying to read his and the nurse's notes to remember me, our meetings and what medications he had me on.

Meetings with Dr. Eren usually lasted up to no more than 10 minutes. He'd ask me how I was feeling. I'd tell him that I'm fine. He'd give me another prescription for my anti-depressant, anti-psychotic and the occasional Xanax for anxiety problems. He was the legal drug dealer who knew how to move you in and out. Give you the drugs you want, collect the money and keep it moving on to the next. There was money to be made and very little time to do it.

Ten minutes with Dr. Eren cost about $250. I didn't know what kind of insurance mom had on file with them, but no one, not even Dr. Eren complained about his money being short. I never complained about the drugs not working for me.

Dr. Eren wasn't one of those doctors who asked you about what could have caused you to have to start taking the anti-this-things and anti-that-things. He only asked how you felt. Sometimes they drew blood. Then send you on your way with your prescriptions. The drug deals worked well. In and out. The quicker the better. No one has time for real questions of truth or the resulting consequences of the truth.

It reminded me of when I saw McKayla selling pills and other things at school. The kids would come up to her. They'd exchange a few words. Then exchange money. In about five to ten minutes, they were gone. Everyone was on their way with what they wanted. The drug dealer had their money and the buyer had his stash. The only difference with this is that Dr. Eren's drug deals were legal and sometimes funded by the state or private insurance.

Although, I did wonder why he never asked me questions about the cause of my depression. I heard that there were other types of doctors who could help me figure it out, but it seemed like it would take more time than just ten minutes every visit. I wasn't too thrilled at the thought of that. But I was curious.

I thought it was because I had diabetes, but I already had medication for diabetes. Diabetes made sense. I knew why I had that. I had been an overweight kid. When I was twelve years old, Mom had put me into sports to try to get me to lose weight. I became very good at soccer, but I kept on getting sick. I felt tired and would get mood swings that were seemingly unmotivated by anything.

One day, in the middle of JV soccer practice, I had passed out. I woke up about a day later. I was told that my blood sugar level had reached over 800. I had no idea what that meant at the time, but I learned later on that it was not good. They told my mom and me that I could have died.

When the doctor told us that I had developed Juvenile Diabetes, I had to start taking insulin. The injections started. Mom could never really get it right. Therefore, I learned how to inject myself without causing too much bruising.

My understanding about diabetes was that my pancreas no longer worked and that I had to lose some weight and take insulin so that my body could process and pass sugar through my body. That made sense to me. As long as I took the insulin, I felt fine physically. However, I didn't understand why I continued to have frequent mood swings. I didn't understand why I felt angry, depressed, manic and altogether emotionally unbalanced without the anti-whatever-pills.

Mom had brought me to Dr. Eren after my last day of playing soccer. Mom made me quit a few weeks after I was diagnosed with diabetes. It was just in time for tryouts for the school's league. This meant, no more Junior Varsity! I could go on to play *real* soccer. She was scared that it wasn't safe for me to play.

That day, I did something that I had never done before. I got physically violent. Mom told me that I couldn't play soccer anymore and I felt a sudden rage. I picked up my notebook and slapped her across the face with it.

At first, she didn't know what to do. She stared at me, stunned. She didn't get angry. Instead, she cried. She walked away from me. I went without dinner that night.

The incident that made her start bringing me to Dr. Eren occurred on the first day that I had ever felt that I couldn't get out of bed. One morning, mom tried to wake me up to get ready for school. My body ached and inside I felt as if I was on fire. However, mom said that I didn't have a fever. She checked my temperature and it was 96 degrees Fahrenheit. It was normal. My head ached and mom gave me Tylenol. The headache didn't go away.

At the time, my father was living with us. He

thought that a walk in the park would do me some good. I agreed to go. With all of my strength, which seemed very little, I trudged beside him. Before going to the park, my father stopped by a package store. I waited outside for him. It only took him about five minutes to go in, buy his liquor, and come back out. He walked out of the store with a brown paper bag. He put the bag to his lips and began drinking from whatever container that was inside of that paper bag.

As we walked in the park, we looked at the grass and talked about how blue the sky was and everything seemed normal. I remember seeing a man jogging beside a German Shepard. The man didn't have his dog on a leash. I thought that was strange.

Something happened between that liquor store, the walk in the park, the German Shepard and my father not coming home.

Suddenly, I was at home. My father was not at home with me. I stood alone, in the living room of my house. I remember screaming at the top of my lungs. Whatever I was screaming, it was unintelligible. I can't remember what I had said. I screamed so loudly that the cacophony of my cries made my ears ache in pain. I picked up a photo of mom, my father and I and I threw it across the room. I picked up mom's vase of roses that my father had given her the day before and I threw them at the television, causing it to break the vase, spill water all over the floor and crack the television screen. I went on like that, tearing up the living room. They had left me alone in that room until my mother found me, sprawled out on the floor, not moving. Mom had said that seeing me on the floor scared her. She had said that I had looked gray and drained of life. She had been scared and furious.

"What did you do?" She yelled at me.

I was stoic. Silent. Unmoved.

She shook me by my shoulders and yelled, "You've made a complete mess of everything. Do you know that? I can't believe this!"

I remember her storming out of the room and leaving me to lay in the middle of broken glass, dust and smelly liquids that drained from broken containers.

Shortly, she returned with a bucket filled with hot water and a bottle of bleach. She screamed, "You will clean up this mess! Do you hear me, Daniel? You will clean this room until it sparkles. Your father will be home tonight. I know he will. He's coming home, don't you worry. And when he gets here, he will want to see everything back as it was. Don't stop cleaning until this room is spotless!"

I picked up the scrub brush that floated in the bucket and began to sweep up the glass. Then I took a towel and poured bleach onto it. The smell of the bleach filled my nostrils and a sudden pain shot through my nasal passage and caused a tingle in my brain. It was kind of like the feeling you get when you eat good wasabi. I liked it.

I believed my mom when she said that my father would be home that night. Why wouldn't he? We went to the package store, walked to the park, I petted a man's unleashed German Shepard and then...I was scrubbing my living room waiting for my father to come home. However, no matter how much I believed Mom, scrubbed the floor, poured bleach and scrubbed some more, my father didn't come home that night.

I looked down at my right arm as I wiped the floor. There was a bite mark. It left a mild, red spot. It was a small bite. It didn't look like the skin had been broken. It didn't really hurt.

By the time Mom came back into the living room, everything was cleaned up. The photograph of us was intact, but the glass had shattered. There was still a crack in the television screen, but it could be repaired. Mom marveled.

She said with a slight giggle, "You do this better than me."

I smiled at her because she was smiling. When she smiled, it lit up the room. Her plump and freckled cheeks bunch up under green eyes. She shook her head and her reddish brown hair brushed like silk up against her shoulders. She reached out her arms to me and I ran into them. She embraced me tightly. I still hung on to the dripping wet, bleached towel and the scrub brush. Water and bleach dripped onto the hardwood floor. Mom didn't care. She cried as she kissed the top of my head. My black, curly and wild hair pulled back as she brushed it with her hands and squatted down to look at me.

"Your father will be happy. You've fixed what can be fixed for now. Somehow, we'll fix that television and anything else that's broken."

The television got fixed. We bought a new picture frame for the photo. Mom bought a new vase, but she put it in the china cabinet with all of her other fancy glasses, crystal and chinaware. I guess she didn't want to put new flowers in it just yet. She had said that we would fix what had been broken. Perhaps that's why I saw Dr. Eren? Maybe I was broken in some kind of way.

Again, it made sense physically. My pancreas was broken. It didn't work. Therefore, insulin helped me pass sugar the way it would normally if my pancreas did work. But Mom made me start seeing Dr. Eren for medication after I had messed up the living room and my father didn't come home after our walk in the park, as she had said he would.

"I'm good," I told Dr. Eren.

"Excellent," he replied. "The medications are working for you. We'll keep it up at the same doses that we have you on. I don't see a need to increase or decrease anything, as you didn't report any severe side effects. I don't see any changes in your eating habits and weight. Dr. Taylor, from the clinic, sent me the update on your regular, physical check ups. He says you've been regularly taking your insulin, eating well and maintaining your physical health. Are you still active?"

"What?" I asked.

"It says here in your chart that you had played soccer. Are you still active at your school?"

"Sure," I lied. "We practice almost every day."

His face seemed to light up. He said, "I've heard good things about your school. The blue and gold! You must be excited about the championships that are coming up."

I rolled my eyes to the ceiling and tightly gripped the edges of the chair where I was sitting. I held my breath so that I would not scream. I felt the anger wanting to burst out of me.

Dr. Eren scribbled something on a pad and ripped it out of his notebook. He held the piece of paper out to me.

"Give this to Nurse DeCosta and she'll call in your prescription, but you'll still need to hold on to that to pick it up from your pharmacy."

I jumped up out of the chair, grabbed the

prescription note from him and hurried out the door. I checked in with Nurse DeCosta. She was a beautiful woman with long dark brown hair, tanned skin and perfectly manicured nails that you only thought movie stars could afford. She smiled at me as she took the prescription out of my hands.

"Are you still using the Kroger Pharmacy on Javick Road to fill your prescriptions?" She asked with a perfectly white, enameled smile.

I smiled back at her and leaned towards her with my elbows propped up on the counter where she sat behind in a swirly, leather chair. I felt my heart rate speed up again, but not with anger this time.

"Yes," I said.

She spun around in her chair and typed on her computer. About ten seconds later she turned back towards me, handed me my prescription note and said, "You're all set, darling. We'll see you in four weeks."

Hehe, she called me darling.

"Okay," I said.

CHAPTER 10

I didn't realize how long it took to get home from the doctor's office when I took the train and the bus. A trip that should only take about 15 minutes driving in the car with my mom, took about 2 hours on public transit.

Whenever I rode public transit, I survived those rides by pretending like I was at an art exhibit. I was merely an observing student, there to study.

People were like artistic creations. Our transportation was the gallery and the energy that we possessed and released were our canvases. We received what was put out into the world. There were many different mediums of art in the gallery. Some people looked like you could assume where they were coming from or where they were going. That would determine the price and value of each art piece.

Take for example, the people who seemed to stand on the "right wing" of the train. There was a dapper man who stood close by the train doors. He never sat down because he didn't want to wrinkle his dark gray, dry cleaned and neatly pressed suit. He stood by the exit door and stared into the window, rather than out of the window because he was looking at his own reflection.

Occasionally, he picked a booger from his nose

and flung it away as if it was a foreign object. Then he ran his fingers through his slicked back hard gelled hair and shifted his tie. Satisfied with himself, he smiled and turned away from his reflection in the train window. He was definitely on his way to the office to make another dollar.

"You've got to put in the time to make an extra dime," Tom once said to me when he tried to encourage me to get an after school job.

At the next stop on the train, entered the thirty-something-year-old looking woman. She was dressed in her posh, pink and blue yoga pants and a light gray pull over sweater. She pushed her baby stroller onto the train with a diaper bag on one shoulder and a yoga mat in its own bag, strapped over her other shoulder.

Surely, she would have sat down if there was enough room or if a kind gentleman would have given up his seat for her. Rather, it seemed that she preferred to stand up in order to get in a pre-stretch before yoga class. She held onto her baby stroller with her left hand, gripping the handle in such a way that you couldn't miss the *Tiffany* diamond ring on her wedding finger.

Using the baby stroller for balance, she bent over and stretched her legs. This caused the man in the dark gray suit to sneak a peak at her yoga toned, motherly plumped ass. And of course, like a tease, as soon as the train stopped, she gathered herself and rushed off the train with her baby in the stroller, her yoga mat, the diaper bag and everything else her husband was paying for.

She didn't want to miss her yoga class. She has to stay healthy and looking fit so that hubby would find her attractive enough to want to make babies numbers 2.5

with her.

"You've got to work hard to have a happy All-American family and home," Tom tried to drill into my head after I had vocally resented getting a job.

"Living the dream," is what he called it.

However, on the other side of the train were different types of pieces of work. They were the ones that the man in the business suit and the yoga mom tried to keep their distances.

The art on the other side of the train is the kind of art that you can't simply buy like the ones on the right side. I found those people to be priceless. Why? Because on the opposite end were beggars, panhandlers, shopping cart women and the homeless. They are the people who live their lives day by day. They work for their survival in a way that others could not buy for them or from them.

A panhandler dressed in torn brown pants and a mildew smelling navy blue sweater walked by me with his dirty hands stretched out. He asked for some spare change so that he could get something to eat. I reached into my pocket and found 75 cents. I gave it to him. The lady, who sat next to me, reached into her purse and pulled out a sandwich that was wrapped in plastic and gave it to him.

"Thank you. God bless you," he said to us with a nod and thankful smile.

Then the panhandler approached the man in the dark gray suit just as he was turning away from the yoga mom who had just left the train. The train doors closed and the man in the gray suit turned around to see the panhandler standing next to him.

Mr. Panhandler reached out his hand to Mr. Dark Gray Suit and asked him for his spare change. Mr. Dark

Gray Suit quickly turned his head away from Mr. Panhandler. He sniffed up another booger and shook his head without giving Mr. Panhandler another moment of his precious time.

Graciously, Mr. Panhandler said to Mr. Dark Gray Suit, "Thank you anyway and may God bless you." Then he lifted his chin and kept on moving, making his way down the aisle to continue his job, panhandling to survive another day.

This was a perfect example of priceless art and junk art. Mr. Panhandler was priceless art. He worked for his life. He didn't flinch, cry nor bat an eyelash if someone didn't pay him for his begging time. However, if Mr. Dark Gray suit didn't get his pay on time at the office, or even if his check was a dollar or two short, surely he would have a word or two with the payroll department. He may even complain to his co-workers about the unfair treatment he was receiving from the company that he worked for.

Then there was Yoga Mom. She reminded me of the most junkiest art of them all. Do you think she would give her husband offspring if that *Tiffany* diamond didn't shine as brightly as her newly sculpted, expensive yoga butt?

Mr. Dark Gray Suit and Yoga Mom were buyable, imitation art pieces that you could get anywhere. They had their lives, safety nets, nest eggs (whatever the hell that is), and they knew that they would live to see another day as long as they had a home and something to eat. Those things are guaranteed to them because of who they are while standing on the right side of the train. There were plenty like them and they always stayed in print because they lived long, rich and entitled, privileged lives.

Mr. Panhandler was a limited edition. He lived day by day. If he couldn't afford to eat nor find good shelter, it would mean life or death for him. There wouldn't be another art piece that was like him. Maybe there would be others like him when he's gone, but it wouldn't be *him*.

That was the difference between junk art and priceless art. It was the same difference between those of us who are *people* and those of us who are *human*. To be human, it requires you to have a certain level of humanity that comes from within and it's unselfish. Later on in life, I learned that it also requires a good level of mindfulness. I will tell you about that when we get there.

I only had the level of mindfulness to accept that all of us had different backgrounds, stories and talents. We were all different colors, races, genders, sexes, shapes and sizes. No matter where we came from or where we were going, we all met and meshed aboard the same buses and trains. We were all displayed in the same life gallery.

I tried to remember some of the faces of the people and humans that I crossed paths with so that I could draw them later, when I returned home. I didn't like drawing while I was on the train because people were too nosy. Usually there was not enough room for privacy.

A man who called himself "The Ice Cream Man" came aboard the train at Five Points Train Station as we headed North. He didn't have any ice cream to share with any of us on the train. However, he said that he had a special treat for all of us and he instructed us to "hold up and listen".

The Ice Cream Man began to rap a song in the style of a capella. He rapped to us bystanders an original song that he claimed to have written. The song was called "Big Booty In The Flesh". I liked it. It had an upbeat, fun flow to it. The lyrics were encouraging. He rapped about how to appreciate the rear side of a feminine, shapely woman and the song instructed us listeners on how the woman's ass should be treated in an intimate, lovemaking situation. I could relate to that song!

When he finished with his song, "The Ice Cream Man" passed out flyers to announce when his debut album was "going to drop" and when and where his next show was going taking place. The album release and his next show were not going to be free nor on public transit. I grabbed a flyer from him. And I remembered his face to draw later when I got home.

Along my walk home from the train, I asked to bum a cigarette from a nice lady who was smoking and waiting for a taxi just outside of the train station. She said that her name was Julie. Julie was a hairdresser and she said that she was running late for work. She had a client at 6pm and was afraid that she wouldn't get there on time if she took the bus. Therefore, she opted for a taxi that seemed to be taking just as long as the bus would have taken to get her to work on time.

She said that she liked my curly hair.

"Your hair is crazy!" She commented. "You ever let anyone braid it back for you so that you don't have it all over the place like this?"

I shook my head and smirked.

Then Julie asked if she could touch my hair. I let her touch it as soon as she asked. I had to insure that she'd give me a cigarette. Nonetheless, I had to wait for the cigarette until she finished running her hands through my hair, petting me, and getting her hands into the thick of my curls to make sure that her fingers could go all of the way through it without a tangle. It was awkward, but I let her have her way because I desperately wanted a cigarette.

She asked me weird questions like, "Are you mixed?" and "Are you Hispanic?"

I laughed when people asked me dumb questions about my background. I seemed to be like a puzzle to them. I remember my art teacher once called me, "racially ambiguous" in front of the whole class. It made me laugh.

The kind woman stopped rubbing my hair and reached into her purse. She pulled out her business card, a lighter and a carton of cigarettes. She handed me her business card first and said, "Call me if you want to get your hair braided or twisted. I think it would look nice in twists."

Julie gave me her lighter and a cigarette from her carton of American Spirits. Yuck! I thought to myself. Ah well, beggars can't be choosy. I took the cigarette and lighter. Then I thanked her.

"So, what are you?" She asked as I lit the cigarette with her lighter.

I handed the lighter back to Julie and chuckled. I took a long drag of the cigarette and held in the smoke as I turned away from her and began walking in the direction towards my house.

"I'm human. Thank you! God bless you," I said as a cloud of smoke released from my mouth.

I heard her let out a great belly laugh as I walked away.

CHAPTER 11

When I arrived home, Tom's car was parked in the driveway behind my mom's car. The front door was wide open. I stepped in and looked around confused.

Mom yelled from the kitchen, "Hold on Ma! I'm going to make sure Tom gets all of your stuff inside. Then we can look for your magazines."

Who was she talking to?

"That's fine. I'm not in a hurry," a gentle, womanly voice said from the living room.

I looked into the living room. An elderly woman was sitting on Mom's recliner. She lay back, looking relaxed and content. Boxes and black plastic bags were stacked around the living room. The elderly woman pushed back her long black and gray hair that draped down her light brown shoulders. She wore a floral sundress and thick black stockings. Her brown loafers sat on the floor beside the recliner. As soon as she saw me, she reached out her skinny, brown and wrinkly arms and a warm light came over her face. She seemed to have lit up at the sight of me.

"My baby!" She shouted.

"What did you say, Ma?" Mom asked as she entered the living room from the kitchen.

Mom looked at me, realizing that I was finally home. She didn't look very pleased with me. Surely, Tom told her about my attitude when he had driven me to Dr. Eren's office. I wondered if he told her about how he had scared me to death while he was driving.

"Don't just stand there, give me a hug!" Grandma exclaimed with open arms.

Before I could come any closer, she jumped up off the recliner and leaped into my arms. I had forgotten how tiny Grandma was. She was only 4 feet and ten inches tall. When I was a kid, it had been weird to see her standing next to my father, her son, because he was a giant compared to her. My father stood at six feet and five inches tall. In the back of mind, I used to wonder to myself how she squeezed my Pop out of that tiny body of hers. It didn't occur to me that my father was once a baby and had to grow up to his size. I couldn't envision my Grandma as a baby either. I used to think that Grandmas were put here on Earth for their grandchildren. Like, she was here for me. Grandmothers were put in the world to take care of their grandchildren, feed us, buy us stuff at Christmas and on our Birthdays and give us candy.

When I was six years old, I learned differently. Grandma had told me that she was once a baby. She showed me a photograph of her as an infant. The Baby Grandma lay in a bassinet dressed in a Christening gown and smiling, glowing like a newly baptized baby.

I remember that I didn't take the news very well. I had a moment of "what the fuck" and denied it for a while. I thought that my father, my grandmother and Mom were trying to play some kind of sick joke on me. I'm not sure of validity of this, but Mom once told me that after Grandma showed me the photograph, I seemed to have blacked out for a second. She said that I fell back onto the couch and wasn't responsive. My eyes had been wide open, but I wouldn't respond to anything they were saying until finally, Grandma pinched my arm. Then I began to cry.

I stared at the Baby Grandma photo and literally cried. I don't really remember all of what had happened. However, I do remember the emotion it evoked in me to feel the pain of losing something before it had already been lost. I guess I thought that Grandma would always be Grandma, never to go away. She'd never change or grow any younger or older. She'd be there for me as she was Mom-Mom. Never changing. Never born so that she could never die.

When Mom-Mom leaped into my arms, I caught her with ease. She was light and she smelled like strawberries and coffee. Her smile was like something I had missed for a very long time. When she smiled at me, I felt like I was going to cry for some reason.

"Awww, baby," she said as she pulled away from me and reached her hand up to touch my face. "Don't cry. I'm happy to see you, too."

I hadn't realized I was crying until I felt teardrops falling down my cheeks. The tears clouded up my vision.

"Hi, Mom-Mom," I managed to choke out.

"Look who is finally back at home," my mother said as she entered the living room.

I reached into my pocket and gave my mom my prescription from Dr. Eren. She took it from me and looked at it.

"The nurse called it in," I said. "You just have to pick it up with that."

"Fine," Mom said. "I'll go get your medicine. You

finish helping Tom get Mom-Mom's things into the house. Then I need for you to pack up your room."

That caught me off guard.

"Liz," Mom-Mom said to my mother, "you don't need to push the boy out of his room on account of me. I'll do just fine here on the pull out bed, on the sofa."

I realized what was happening.

"Daniel," my Mom called out to me, "I want you to finish up helping Tom and get to packing up your room so that Mom-Mom can move in."

"Where am I going to sleep?" I asked.

Mom chuckled. She said, "You have some nerve, child. Get your shit packed up and out of the room so that Mom-Mom can move in. What does it matter to you anyway? You like to leave here at night and not return until the next day like you're some kind of alley cat. You want to behave like a feral cat then you will be treated like one. You can keep your clothes in my closet and box up your crap. Use the garage as storage. You can sleep out there with your stuff or in here on the sofa. You will do it and not say another word about it!"

Rage filled my insides until I began to see red. I pushed Mom-Mom so hard that she flew back onto the recliner she had been sitting on. She yelped in pain. Unmoved by Mom-Mom's cry, I stepped up to my mother and put my face close to hers so that she could see how angry I was becoming.

"What?" My mother challenged me.

"NO!" I yelled to her face. "I'm not moving out! You can't make me!"

My mother began to raise her hand and at that moment, Tom came from out of nowhere and pushed me to the ground. I felt the wind fly out of my lungs as soon as I hit the floor. I landed on my back. I tried to get back up, but Tom bent down and pressed his arms and elbows down on my chest, causing sharp pains in my lungs. I couldn't catch my breath, but I was so angry that I didn't care. I thrashed my body around and kicked my legs. Tom jumped on top of me. I felt him pin down my legs with his legs as he pressed down harder on my chest. I swung my arms and began to punch Tom in his face, on his neck and his arms. I fought hard, even though I couldn't breath. I felt myself growing weak and my eyesight began to blur. My chest became full of fire and bile rose in my throat. I let out a shrill cry with what little air I had in my lungs.

"Oh my God! Lord, Jesus! Stop it! You're hurting him!" I heard Mom-Mom cry out.

I stopped fighting and lay my arms down flat on the floor. Tom pressed down on me again to make sure that I had fully submitted. I did not move. My eyes stayed open, fixated on Tom's angry, red face. He gave my chest one last shove and growled at me before he eased up off of me and let me loose.

When the pressure was off of my chest, I inhaled deeply. It was hard to catch enough air in my lungs to be able to exhale again. When I exhaled, I wheezed and coughed. Phlegm and mucus spilled from my mouth and nose. I slowly regained my balance as I stood up from the floor.

"Lord, have mercy!" Mom-Mom said as she grasped at the holy cross that she wore around her neck. "Is he okay? Baby boy, are you okay?"

I nodded because I couldn't speak. I coughed and gasped to try to breathe properly again. Mom-Mom handed me a box of tissues from the table beside the recliner. I blew my nose and looked over at my mother as Tom stood between us.

"You have something that you want to say?" Tom asked me.

"No," I coughed out.

"Try again," Tom demanded.

He stepped out of the way from between my mother and me so that we could stand face to face again. He didn't go far. He stood beside mom, just in case I lost it again.

"I'm sorry. I'll move my stuff out now," I said, staring angrily at Tom, not my mother.

My mom said, "Do it now."

I stepped forward and Tom put his hand on my chest gently. He said, "Don't you ever put your hands on your grandmother or step up to your mother's face like that again. Do you understand?"

I fought the urge to challenge him. It was hard, but I stepped away from him so that he couldn't touch me again and nodded. Without saying a word, I went to my room, or I should say, Mom-Mom's room and slammed the door shut.

It took almost the rest of the evening to throw my things into boxes and bags to move out of my room. Mom-Mom even came into the room to try to convince me to join her, mom and Tom for dinner. I didn't want to eat, especially with Tom there at our table. I couldn't understand why he was always hanging around. He was nothing to us!

"Come on," Mom-Mom pleaded. "You know that you have to eat. Your sugar, honey..."

I put my hand up to stop her from speaking more about my diabetes. I said, "I know Mom-Mom. I'll eat. I just need to finish this up really quick."

I felt manic and didn't want to stop until it was all done. It didn't matter if my sugar felt low. It didn't matter if I was getting hungry. I didn't care. I just wanted it to be over.

Mom-Mom gave up and went back to the dinner table. I saw her pull out her blood glucose meter and her insulin as I was carrying a stack of boxes out to the garage. Mom and Tom looked over at me as if I was supposed to drop the boxes and join them. Forget it, I said to them in my mind.

They watched me as I hauled all of my bags and boxes out to the garage. By the time I had finished, they had finished dinner, Mom-Mom was passed out in front of the television in the living room on the recliner, and my mother was showered, in her pajamas and in the kitchen cleaning up from dinner. More importantly, Tom left and went back to his house, which was next door.

I stumbled into the kitchen, tired and hungry. I knew my sugar was low. Mom had a plate of grilled chicken, mashed potatoes and cooked carrots on the table, set out for me.

"Eat," she said.

I sat down at the table and began to dig into the food. Mom shook her head and sat down in the chair across from me. I didn't look up as I tore into a drumstick and scooped up a spoonful of carrots right after biting into the chicken.

"Slow down," she laughed.

I barely heard her. I kept on eating.

"You're going to choke," she warned.

"What do you care," I said with a stuffed mouth.

"What?" Mom asked.

I swallowed my food, took a drink of water to wash it down and repeated myself so that she could hear me and understand me clearly.

A pained look appeared on her face. "What is that supposed to mean?" She asked.

"You let Tom almost kill me," I said, almost wanting to cry.

"What was I supposed to do? You were going into one of your fits. I could see it. Tom could see it. You even pushed your Mom-Mom."

"I didn't even know about Mom-Mom coming to live with us," I lied.

"Tom and I tried to talk to you, but you wouldn't listen. Instead, you threw a fit, stomped away like a baby and you shut me out. Then you lied to me and decided to stay out all night and worry me sick. These are the consequences, Daniel."

I lowered my head and my throat began to choke up. I coughed, but it didn't help. I couldn't stop coughing because it felt like whatever I was choking on wouldn't come up or go down.

Mom rushed to my side and patted my back until I stopped coughing and could breathe again. "Here," she said as she picked up my glass of water. "Drink some more water. You are shoveling your food into your face as if you haven't eaten in ages."

I drank more of the water and when I put the glass down on the table, I looked at mom to say thank you, but instead, I burst into tears. She rubbed my back and shoulders as I cried.

"I'm sorry, Mom..." I cried. "I'm so sorry."

"I know," she said, still rubbing my back and shoulders. "I know, sweetie." She kissed my hair gently and ran her fingers through it.

I closed my eyes and let the last of my tears fall. I wiped my eyes and my nose with the sleeves of my hoodie and stayed in her arms.

"Maybe," Mom began, "We should see about taking you to a therapist."

I looked up at her surprised. "Another doctor? Why? For what?" My remorse and sadness was suddenly replaced by annoyance and confusion.

She rose up from beside me and walked to the kitchen sink. She pulled a roll of paper towels from the cabinet above the sink and handed them to me.

"Wipe your face," she said.

I tore a few pieces of the paper towels from the roll and blew my nose as she spoke to me.

"A therapist may be able to help you talk things out. There are many changes going on and you could use someone to talk to about it. Don't you think?"

"I don't know what you mean," I said. I was genuinely confused. "You really want me to see another doctor just to have someone to talk to?"

"Don't you want to talk to someone about what's going on?"

"Can't I just talk to you? I talk to my psychiatrist, Dr. Eren and my other doctor, about my diabetes and my *other stuff*. Isn't that enough? What is a therapist going to do?"

"Well, Tom thinks that it may be a good idea for you to..."

I stood up.

"Daniel, please calm down," Mom pleaded. "Sit down."

"I am calm," I said. "I really don't think that Tom

knows what he is talking about. I don't need another doctor. I take my medicine. I'm going to school and I'm not getting into trouble anymore. I'm almost off academic probation and I'm going to do my best not to make you and Mom-Mom mad at me. I promise."

"You promise not to stay out all night again? You promise not to scare me like you did last weekend?"

"Yes, Mom. I promise." I really meant it when I said it.

"Okay," she said. She hesitated as she stepped forward, but she reached her arms out to me and wrapped them around my waist. I hugged her back.

"You're a good boy, Daniel. Stay that way. Don't change up on me now that you have a girlfriend."

I laughed and blushed.

"It's fine," my mom said as she looked up at me. "Next time I see her, though, I'd like for you both to be dressed and not running around my house half naked again."

We both laughed and I wrapped my arms around her to hug her again.

"Sure, Mom," I said, chuckling. I pulled away from her and began to clean up after myself.

That's how we were when it was just Mom and I. We understood each other. Without Tom and without my Pop, we learned to compromise. She even gave up drinking when my father was put away. Mom and Pop both were heavy drinkers when they were together. It went on for as long as I could remember from when I was a kid.

There was a time when my Mom didn't know how to live without Pop. When he was first put in jail, she broke down. Mom drank even more. She almost lost her job because she became depressed and she didn't go to work. She stopped feeding us, and, at that time, I didn't have diabetes. I used to go to E.J.'s house and eat as much as I could in case Mom didn't go shopping or cook any food. I was a little overweight back then. However, when my Pop got out of jail that first time, and came back home, my mom got her act together again.

My Pop had hard strength about him that held Mom up by the back of her neck. It seemed like she didn't know how to function without him until she was forced to do so after Pop was put in prison this last time. She knew that he wasn't going to get out of prison for a while. We had to come to a compromise. I promised to eat better and to take my medication regularly as to not cause her any distress. She promised me that she would stop drinking. It seemed easy for her to stop drinking when my father was locked up in prison. She didn't have an influence to trigger her into taking to the bottle again. She only had me. That seemed to be enough motivation for her to stop drinking.

It was hard on Mom. She made it clear to me when she would constantly scold me for neglecting to take my medicine. I understood her difficult position. She had an overweight son who she had to get into shape. That's when I started playing soccer.

I learned to play soccer really well. It was fun to exercise with a team and feel proud of accomplishing something. It made me happy. I started to lose weight. I had made many friends when I was playing soccer. Then I got sick.

My mom and I made ourselves strong, together, after I was diagnosed with diabetes. I made myself stronger when I learned how to take care of my diabetes.

Bi-Polar Depression didn't make things easier on us. And my mom left it up to me to take my medication regularly. No one ever talked about a therapist. It hadn't been brought up until the conversation that Mom and I had in the kitchen. It wasn't until Tom butted in and started putting things into Mom's head.

I didn't understand Tom or his intentions. Actually, I didn't *want* to understand Tom. He was a bother to us and he annoyed me. I hated that he was always around and Mom was starting to rely on him like she used to lean on my Pop when he was here. We had already learned to survive, just the two of us. I couldn't let Tom ruin what we had worked hard to maintain. No matter what.

CHAPTER 12

I tried to help Mom-Mom move into my room the next morning. She had slept on the recliner all night in front of the television. She fell asleep after dinner to re-runs of *I Love Lucy* on TV Land. I figured that the network was running an all night marathon of *Lucy*.

I watched Mom-Mom as she rested peacefully with her arms at her sides and her head bowed down. Her long hair draped down her shoulders and bordered her warm, colorful face. She looked graceful when she slept.

I reached for the remote control to turn the television off. I tried to be as quiet and gentle in my movement as to not wake her up yet. The remote control sat beside Mom-Mom on the table next to the recliner and sofa. As soon as I was about to pick it up, I felt Mom-Mom's hand on top of mine.

"Don't touch that," she scolded me. "I am watching this program."

Everybody's grandmother does that, right? I stepped back and looked at her. Just a minute ago, she looked sound asleep. I couldn't comprehend how she knew that I was even there.

"I thought you were asleep, Mom-Mom," I said.

"I was just taking a cat-nap," she said as she

snatched up the remote control and began flipping through the channels.

I laughed and sat down on the sofa beside her.

"Where's your mother?" Mom-Mom asked.

I shrugged my shoulders.

"Well, is her car out there?"

I looked out of the window from where I was sitting. The blinds were open. It looked like my mom had left to go somewhere. Her car wasn't there.

"Nope," I responded.

"I hope that if she went to the store, she'll get my ice cream. I told Liz to not forget my ice cream."

I smiled at Mom-Mom. I loved ice cream, too. Even though I didn't get to eat it as much, I still loved it, just like Mom-Mom.

"I hope she gets some, too," I told Mom-Mom.

Mom-Mom looked at me as if she was puzzled. Then she looked back at the television that was showing a commercial for a new cellular phone that was going to be released in the next three days by the popular brand that had a cult following bigger than anything I'd ever be able to comprehend. The people that went crazy over the new technology by these guys really took a bite out of whatever fruit they produced from their garden variety of shiny new toys for the young and hip.

"Are you going to get one of those new 8.7 or number 10's or whatever they are called?" Mom-Mom asked me.

I couldn't help it. I laughed aloud.

"What is so funny?" She asked. "Isn't that what is *cool* these days?"

Still laughing, I said, "Yes, Mom-Mom. My friend E.J. is going to get one. I probably won't be able to get one though. I have a phone already. Mom bought me one on my last birthday. I am okay with that."

"On your birthday? That was almost a year ago. Don't you need a new one? Like that one?" She pointed to the television.

On television, a young man in a pair of black skinny jeans, a white and blue collared shirt and a pair of the new hipster sneakers spoke on his new phone by the cult and was laughing and smiling. He hung up his phone and began texting as he walked down a street. He turned a corner and suddenly a pretty model type girl with a big smile and big bright eyes who was also texting on her phone met him. They made eye contact, looked happy to see one another, and hugged. Then they walked down the street together and texted some more on their new shiny toys.

By the end of the commercial, three guys and four women had joined the young man in the skinny jeans. They all found themselves in a world together of people that they didn't know, but seemed to know, from all of the love-bombing hugs that they gave each other, but they all went back to looking down at their phones! They met up, hugged and went back to texting. Suddenly, the garden variety logo popped up on the screen and the slogan read "Get Connected!"

I shook my head and found myself laughing even harder. Mom-Mom looked at me again. She seemed puzzled.

"What is so funny?" she asked.

"What was that commercial selling?" I asked.

"A phone! The new phone that you kids are so crazy about these days. Don't you want one, baby?"

I laughed harder, so hard. In fact, a couple of tears

came out of my eyes.

"Mom-Mom, they got phones and met up with their friends, but none of them put their phones away once they met up with each other. They want to sell a phone that helps you connect with your friends, but once you do, you don't even look at them, talk to them, give a real hug or anything and sit down with each other. You just go back to the phone! 'Stay Connected!? How?"

I continued to laugh as Mom-Mom looked at me dubiously.

"I hate to say this," Mom-Mom said. "But your mother was right."

"About what?" I said with one last chuckle.

"You are a bit off," Mom-Mom admitted.

I stopped laughing and turned away from her.

"I didn't mean anything by it," Mom-Mom confessed. "It's just that, most kids your age like stuff like that and they're out with friends and being connected through social media. They take pictures and talk to each other by texting. Yes, I know what texting is. You don't seem to do any of that stuff. Although, she did tell me about that little girlfriend of yours." Mom-Mom observed.

"How much have you talked to Mom and Tom about me?" I asked her.

Mom-Mom shook her head. "You know, it's time for me to take my insulin." Mom-Mom pulled herself up from the recliner, stood up and cracked her bones as she stretched. I cringed as I heard her neck bones and arms and legs make the pop, crack and snap sounds. She was so tiny and old. It scared me to recognize how frail she could have been in her eighty-four years of life. She was beautiful in a graceful way. She went into the kitchen and quickly returned with her insulin and a syringe.

"Aren't you going to check your sugar?" I asked.

"Baby, when you get to be my age, you don't need that damn meter anymore. You just know," she said.

She loaded the syringe with her 70/30 medication and, just like I do, with ease and as if was nothing, stuck the needle into her forearm, pushed the insulin in and took the needle out. I flinched a bit when I saw her pierce her delicate skin. Is that what mom and Tom felt like when they watched me do the same thing?

"So," Mom-Mom said as she bagged her syringe in a zip-lock bag and began to box her insulin away. "Aren't you supposed to be at school?"

"It's only seven o'clock, Mom-Mom," I said. "I don't have to be there until eight o'clock. That's when the home room bell rings."

"Don't you have a bus to catch?" Mom-Mom asked.

Before I could answer, my mom walked through the door with a bunch of grocery bags. It looked like she was struggling as she crashed through the door. I jumped up to help her, but suddenly felt dizzy. Nonetheless, I grabbed a few bags for her and helped carry them into the kitchen.

"Thank you, Daniel," my mom said. She sounded out of breath.

"No problem. Are you okay?"

"Yes," she said.

"Are there anymore bags in the car?"

"No, that's all. Go get ready for school. You can't miss your bus."

"Can I get a ride?" I asked.

"Daniel, you know I have to be at work by nine

o'clock. Why are you asking for a ride now?"

"I am not feeling well," I told her. "I think that I need a minute to not rush this morning."

My mom never denied me when I told her that I wasn't feeling well. It stemmed back from when I was kid and when I first was diagnosed with Diabetes. I think she somehow felt responsible for it. I never reassured her of anything. I just let her feel the way she wanted to feel and think whatever she wanted to think.

"Okay," she sighed. "Fine. But be ready by 7:45. No later than that!"

I smiled, relieved and nodded at her.

"Here," she said as she reached into one of the grocery bags and pulled out two bags from the local pharmacy. She handed the bags to me.

"There is your insulin and the other is your..."

"I know. I know. Thanks, Mom."

I took the bags from her and sat one of them down on the table. I reached into the other bag and pulled out my insulin. I put the vials of insulin in the refrigerator a shelf down from where Mom-Mom kept hers. I didn't want us to get our medications mixed up because we were on different scales. I took out the last vial of insulin from the refrigerator and grabbed a syringe and my bag with my blood glucose meter from one of the cabinets. I started to walk out of the kitchen.

"Excuse me," my mom said.

I turned around to her. She held out the other bag that I had left on the table. She shook it at me. I snatched it from her and walked back into the living room where Mom-Mom was now engrossed in a reality show about women who drank cocktails, gossiped and bragged about having rich husbands and getting tummy tucks and Botox

135

injections.

Mom-Mom looked bemused. She said, "My goodness! If only they had a thing like that when I was that young. I could still look almost like those girls."

"First of all," I said to Mom-Mom as I sat down on the sofa. I opened my bag and pulled out my blood glucose meter and alcohol wipes. "Those women aren't girls. They are old. They look like that because they aren't real. They're fake."

Mom-Mom looked at me shocked. "You're kidding!"

"No, Mom-Mom. It says reality TV, but it's not real. Secondly, by the time those women get to be your age, they'll look much older than they actually are because they messed with the nature of things. You look beautiful just the way you are Mom-Mom because you didn't mess around with that fake stuff."

Mom-Mom shook her head and laughed at me. "You are just like your father, aren't you?" She had a look on her face that made me think that she wanted to reach out and pinch my cheeks. I backed away just in case. "A smooth talking, little heart breaker," she concluded.

"I don't know," I said and shrugged my shoulders. Then I pricked my finger and let the blood drip onto the meter strip. As I had figured, my sugar was high, so I began to prepare my syringe to inject myself with insulin.

Mom-Mom watched me with a frown on her face.

"You still have to take your insulin?" It sounded like a question, but also like a statement as she spoke with sorrow in her quivery voice.

"Yes, Mom-Mom. That's what I'm doing right now."

I loaded the syringe and tapped it to release the bubbles.

"Oh, yea, you got sugar like me and your father. My momma had it too. Seems like everybody in our family get it when we are young. You'll learn to live with it, though. You just have to take good care of yourself. You have to do better than what your father has done."

At that point, I wasn't sure if we were still talking about the Diabetes when she made the final comment about my father.

"What's in the other paper bag?" Mom-Mom asked, pointing at the other bag beside me.

I shook my head.

"Oh," Mom-Mom bellowed. "What about that other medicine your momma had you on?

"What?" I said. "My anti-depressants?"

"Yeah, them things," she said with disdain.

"Yes, Mom-Mom. I still take that medicine, too." It was hard to explain. I had hoped that she would stop questioning me about it.

"For what?" Mom-Mom pressed on me. "What you need those pills for?"

After I had taken my insulin, I put the syringe down and began packing up my things as I spoke to her. "It's for my Bi-Polar Disorder."

"What does that mean? I don't know what that is."

I took a deep breath. Here goes...

"I have depression. It's a mental illness. Kind of like how we have diabetes and it's a physical illness, but if I don't take my medicine, it can kill me. It's the same with depression. If I don't take it, something bad can happen, too."

At that moment, Mom-Mom began to laugh. I was

taken aback.

"Oh Lord. Child," she said with a smile. "What you got to be depressed about? Your life is just beginning. You're just a baby. What you got to be depressed about? You don't pay no bills. You don't have to work no jobs if you don't want to and you have your momma taking care of you. Just tell me, what has got you so depressed that you have to take medication?"

Silently, I hung my head low. I finished packing my things and sat them aside, waiting for more questioning from Mom-Mom. Instead, she seemed to be waiting for me to answer her questions.

"I guess," I struggled to say, "It's like I'm sad sometimes and angry sometimes and it makes me say or do bad things. I feel sick inside of myself sometimes. Like how I feel sick when my sugar is high or low, my anger and sadness can do the same thing. It goes up high when I'm feeling manic. Then it gets low and I'm so depressed that I can't move sometimes. You can see the physical illness because there's a meter to monitor my sugar. But there isn't a meter for me to test my depression. It just happens. So, I have to take medication so that it doesn't kill me, I guess. It's invisible, because it's inside of me and you can only see it when it gets bad. When I act out it comes out emotionally. The medicine keeps me from doing that."

I thought back to the day before when I had pushed Mom-Mom. The way she was staring at me as I tried my best to explain it to her made me think that she thought that I was talking a different language. She looked puzzled and unconvinced.

I was going to take my other medicine there, but Mom-Mom made me think twice about it with her dubious stare. I began to get up to go to the kitchen, but she stopped me as she began to speak.

"You don't need no pills for sadness," Mom-Mom reasoned. "The problem is that you need Jesus."

I felt my eyes grow big. I was *not* expecting that!

"There ain't no such thing as mental illness. There's only what is real. There's what you can see. It's like what you said about those girls on TV with the fake lips and hair that makes them look young like that, but they ain't young. It ain't real, baby. It's not like Diabetes. I know what I'm talking about. Now, I've had sugar for over fifty years. I was young like you when I got it. I dealt with it just fine like I do now. You're just a child. Ain't even had a chance to grow up and see what the real world is like. You don't know what it's like to have your own responsibilities and live on your own. So, again, what you got to be sad about?"

I was defeated. "I don't know, Mom-Mom."

"Then if you don't know, you don't need to be sad. You are too young to be sad. Change your thinking now, while you're still a child. And just be happy!" She smiled at me sincerely as she told me to be happy. I knew she meant it to be kind, but it stung me painfully somewhere inside.

"Listen," she said as she leaned in closer to me. She lowered her voice and looked around as if to make sure no one else could hear her, but me. "I know your daddy did some bad things. That is sad. The situation is sad. And he got himself into his own mess because he didn't change his thinking when he was young. He was caught up in things he wasn't supposed to do. I am not going to let you go down the same road your father chose. Although, it's not too late for him to be saved, he still has a chance, and so do you. God knows, I tried with him. He is my son. Therefore, I forgave him. The Lord showed me how to forgive and you need to do the same thing. Forgive and forget, as Jesus taught us by his example when He forgave the man who was a murderer and a thief who hung beside Our Lord on the cross beside him before He died. Once you forgive your father, you will find that there is nothing to be sad about."

I was speechless. No one had ever spoken to me like the way she had spoken. I had never read the Bible. I had heard of Jesus. But I didn't understand how He had anything to do with my Diabetes nor my depression. I tried to get up to leave, but Mom-Mom kept on talking to me.

"Your daddy will be home soon and you'll have a chance to have your family back together again. It probably does make you sad sometimes to think about your daddy being gone, but he will be back soon. Just stop thinking about the bad things and look towards your bright future."

Mom-Mom picked up my bag of medicine with my anti-depressants in it. She looked at one of the bottles and tossed it back into the bag. She threw the bag at me. It hit me on my stomach and fell to the floor.

Mom-Mom scowled and said, "And stop taking those damn pills!" She seemed to snap from peaceful preaching Mom-Mom to an angry old hag in just a second.

"You don't need that shit!"

I lightly gasped. I had never heard Mom-Mom say the "S" word before.

"That shit is poison! That's probably what's making you feel bad. It probably messes with your sugar, too. I'm going to talk to your momma about that shit!"

I found myself covering my ears like a five year old by the time she finished speaking. I must've looked frightened because her face softened and she reached out to me.

"I'm sorry baby," Mom-Mom said. "I just don't want to see you sad. I love you."

"I love you too, Mom-Mom," I said as I picked up my bag of medicine from the floor.

"I tell you what," she said as she reached her little arms out to me.

I did not step closer to her. She was clearly not okay even though she seemed to be calmer than before. At least her "S" bombs stopped torpedoing at me. I had never seen an old woman go from speaking about Jesus so genuinely and sincerely and in the same breath start cursing someone out in such a vulgar way. She just seemed to snap in and then snap back out again. She reminded me of when I am around Tom.

"How about you come to church with me this weekend?" Mom-Mom said with a gentle smile. "You will get the right kind of spiritual food that will lift you up and take away all of that sadness."

"I don't know," I said as I started to walk away.

"Pray about it," she shouted as I left the room.

"Sure, Mom-Mom. Your room is ready. It's all yours," I shouted as I walked towards the garage, my new home.

I threw away the empty insulin vial and the syringe in a waste basket beside the futon that was now my bed. I plopped down onto the futon and tried to take in everything that had just happened. Maybe Mom-Mom was right, I thought. Mental illness never made sense to me the way that Diabetes made sense. It was hard to explain to Mom-Mom, let alone explain to myself. I looked at the bag that contained my anti-depressants. It took me a moment of contemplation before I had the nerve to take out the two bottles of pills.

I stood up and held one of the bottles in my hand. I pretended to dribble the bottle like it was a basketball.

"Three points to win the game," I said, mimicking a sports announcer's voice. I threw the bottle of pills and it landed in the waste basket on top of the used syringe.

"Oh! It's in! Only two points and thirty seconds to go on the clock!" I said. "Well, Dave, Danny Boy's got one more shot before the clock runs out. Let's see if he has it in him to make that last shot. Can he do it?" I spun around, ran up to the basket and tossed the last bottle of medicine in the basket.

"He dunked it! Did you see that Dave? He dunked it in right at the last second. Danny Boy beat the shit out of Depression! Looks like that kid is going places, Dave. He's going to be alright."

I ran around the garage and threw my hands into the air, pretending to give high fives to imaginary fans and teammates while making fake crowd cheers. Then I stopped beside the waste basket. I looked into it one last time and tied up the bag. I opened the garage door and carried the bag to the corner, where the garbage men picked up our waste. Just in time, I thought to myself as the garbage truck pulled up. Two big men jumped off the back of the truck and said hello. They took the bag from me and grabbed the other garbage. Then they dumped all of it into the truck. I thanked them and headed back to the garage.

Mom was suddenly standing next to my futon. She

looked confused.

"Since when did you start taking out the garbage?" Mom asked in a smart aleck tone. She put her hands on her chubby hips and cocked her head at me.

I said, "You're welcome."

She laughed and shouted as she walked into the house, "Hurry up and get dressed. Don't forget to take your medicine before we go."

"I already did!" I yelled.

CHAPTER 13

By the time homeroom bell rang, I wanted to kill someone. Mainly, I wanted to kill Rex King. Rex King was the guy that made Ryan look like a bitch. Many people liked Ryan for obvious reasons, but Rex King had many traits about him that made him...well...I guess "king" of the school. No pun intended.

I had first met Rex King when we were in JV soccer together. He was short, scrawny and shy back then. His father was one of the parent coaches in our school. I could tell that Rex seemed to have something big to prove to everyone who was watching him.

Rex King became one of the great ones when it came to grade school soccer. He became so skilled at soccer, that I had felt moved to ask him to show me some of the tricks on the field. At that time, he didn't mind showing me some moves. After all, we were on the same team.

Rex had mastered numerous moves such as how to do a banana kick, back heel and a back pass. He used to do a power move. He would thrust his body back, almost like he was going to do a back flip and kick the ball high into the air. Then he jumped up into the air in one swift movement with his legs swooping into the air. Moving the ball from one leg to the other, the ball would bounce into the air swiftly. With enough velocity, the ball would fly over his legs and all of the rest of our heads and this final kick made it into the goal. He never missed when he did that trick.

As I watched him from the back of Mr. Blankenship's classroom, I thought of ways to steal his blue and gold jacket.

He sat up from with his friends, laughing, joking and talking about stupid things that had nothing to do with anything and pretended that there wasn't anything more important than them in the world.

Rex caught me glaring at him and the smile that he had had on his face disappeared. It was replaced by a hard grin. He mouthed something to me that was inaudible. However, I could slightly make out what his message was as his upper lip bit down lightly on his lower lip. Then he opened his mouth slightly, but not widely. The back of his tongue touched the upper part of his mouth, still while his mouth was open. He paused for a moment. Then he closed his mouth a little, opened it again by pushing his tongue forward causing his lips to make an exaggerated O shape into a puckered up kind of kiss.

I stood up and shouted, "Fuck you, too!"

Mr. Blankenship, who had been in the middle of doing role call for homeroom, stopped calling out names. My colleagues began to laugh and stared right at me. I became embarrassed, as I had forgotten where I was for a moment.

CHAPTER 14

"Daniel, why are we here, again?" My guidance counselor asked.

He sat behind his desk that was covered in pink slips, white paper with stupid words on them that got kids into trouble and worst of all, what I was faced with, academic probationer warning slips.

Our school's guidance counselor, Mr. Barry Wolff, was a late twenty something year old, hipster looking guy. He wore horn-rimmed, black glasses, a white button down, short-sleeved shirt with a silver and black skinny tie around the collar. And he wore black, well-fitted slacks. Suspenders held up his pants. The suspenders were decorated with tiny silver skulls stitched onto the finely tailored looking fabric. His mousy, blonde hair was parted at the side and slicked back behind his ears. I had no idea exactly how old he was. However, he looked like he could have been one of my classmates.

Mr. Wolff gave me a strange feeling because he had the power to reprimand me, yet, he looked like he could have been one of my classmates. It didn't help that he often spoke in questions. He didn't really talk to me by giving me clear answers. I guess it was supposed to make me think, but it made me feel confused. This was my second time in his office. The first time, was when I got put on academic probation. This time is my second warning. If I received a third warning, then I would be kicked out. Which never made sense to me because if the first time you are called into the guidance counselor's office and it is supposed to be a warning, then why are you suspended? Also, why is the third visit considered a warning when at that point they kick you out anyway? Shouldn't the second visit, the one I am at now, be considered the first warning? Shouldn't I get two more chances if there are supposed to be three warnings?

"You know, it's three strikes and you're out, right?" Mr. Wolff had asked.

I shook my head.

"Am I going to have to call your mother, Daniel?"

"Is it up to me if you call my mom, or...?

"What do you think, Daniel?"

What is my life? I thought to myself.

"No? Yes?" he asked.

I took a deep breath and said, "No. I will go to class and take this as my final warning before I get suspended again."

"Okay," Mr. Wolff said. He put a round, peppermint candy into his mouth sucked on it for a bit. "Also, do you think that you should apologize to Mr. King, Mr. Blankenship and the rest of your homeroom class?"

"No," I confessed, resenting the order he had put his priority list in for apologies.

Mr. Wolff raised his eyebrows. I waited for him to ask another question. I almost had hoped that he would actually demand that I apologize. I would have even considered standing in front of homeroom and apologizing to each and every one of my colleagues if he had said something even remotely inspiring.

Instead, he asked, "Are you sure about that?"

I nodded.

"Ah well," he sighed as he picked up a ceramic coffee travel mug that was adorned with the green and white logo of the popular coffee house chain that fed the caffeine fiends of the world. It had the sippy-cup top that reminded me of the cups that I had once drank out of when I was a toddler before I could drink out of regular cups without lids.

"This is your second warning, Daniel. Will I see you back in here next time for expulsion?"

I stood up, gathered my books and shook my head. Mr. Wolff took a sip of his fancy coffee. He let out a great sigh as he sat his mug down and smiled at me.

"I sure hope not. You do know that you have so much more potential to succeed, don't you, Daniel?"

I chuckled, amused at his question. He couldn't say. Therefore, he had to ask me.

"Sure," I laughed. "Can I go now?"

"Is there anything else that you want to talk about?"

I held back my laughter and shook my head.

"Are you sure, Daniel? Is there anything that you need to talk about? Get off of your chest?"

"Is there anything that you need to talk about, Mr. Wolff?" I couldn't resist. Therefore, I laughed.

Mr. Wolff must've taken my laughter for happiness. He may have felt as if he had gotten through to me. Mr. Wolff laughed, too in high pitched and snorty way. I'm not sure what he was laughing at. Perhaps he was laughing because I was laughing. But I was laughing *at him*. Mr. Wolff didn't seem like the type of guy who laughed at himself. Therefore, what the hell was he laughing at? The thought made me laugh even harder. I laughed so hard that it made me cough a little.

Sometimes, it amused me when people would take me the wrong way. I do tend to laugh or even smile when I'm upset, confused or scared. Some people would think that I am happy or entertained. However, sometimes, it's the exact opposite. It seemed that Mr. Wolff read me completely wrong on that day.

Mr. Wolff gathered himself as I opened the door to leave. He said, "Daniel, I'm happy that we had a chance to talk today. Do you feel that..."

Here comes the B.S., I thought to myself.

"Do you think that our chat has given you a chance to resolve your anger issues so that you can do better as to not end up getting kicked out of school?"

I nodded again, laughing even harder as I walked out of his office. Quickly, I slipped out of the door and closed it behind me.

I released a huge sigh once I was safely on the other side, away from Mr. Wolff. I sat my books down on the counter of the front desk of the reception area. The secretary, Mrs. Lieberman, looked up at me and addressed me by my first and last name. She knew me well enough. I had been to the counselor's office enough times.

"Sit tight for me, Daniel Blackwell," she said. "I'm going to grab a pass for you so that you can get to your next class."

She went into a room that had a door that she had to use a key to get into. Then she shut the door behind her.

I leaned against the counter, next to my books. I

looked up at the clock. It was almost my lunch period. Wow! I thought to myself, does time really exist?

Just as I was looking away from the clock and turning back to see if Mrs. Lieberman had returned with my pass, a woman walked through the main entrance into the reception area. She had black hair with streaks of blue, pink, orange and green. She was dressed in black ankle boots, a short black skirt, and a white tank top where you could see her purple bra underneath. Her metallic gray and white bracelets looked all too familiar as they dangled from her wrists where I noticed scars that I had once kissed. I felt myself tingle inside.

"What are you doing here?" The woman asked me.

I stumbled on my words like a dumb ass. "I um...there was a thing and Mr. Blankenship sent Mr. Wolff a thing and... I see...you have *hair*."

Theresa giggled. "Yes, I have hair. What about it?"

"Colors...they...you have stuff in your hair. You have hair." What the hell was wrong me? I couldn't speak.

Theresa walked up to me and reached up. She gripped a chunk of my hair lightly and said, "You have hair, too."

She ran her fingers through my hair, causing butterflies to flutter in my stomach.

"Wha- What are you doing here?" I said as she continued to pet me.

"Doesn't matter," she said. Then she stopped touching me.

"Oh," I sighed.

"Hey, Danny Boy," she said with a smile.

I raised my eyebrows at her in anticipation.

"Can I borrow a cigarette?"

Smiling, knowing and ready, I reached into my pocket and pulled out a pack of Marlboro's that I had swiped from my Mom's purse that morning before she had dropped me off at school.

I opened the carton, and, to my surprise, there were three cigarettes left inside of the carton. I smiled at Theresa and said, "Luckily, I do."

Mrs. Lieberman began turning the knob to return to the reception area. Suddenly, Theresa grabbed my arm and quickly pulled me away. Before Mrs. Lieberman returned, likely to find us gone, Theresa and I were already out of the school building and running away. I laughed as I let her pull me.

"Come on! Move faster!" she shouted as we ran.

Where were we going? I did not know, nor did I care.

CHAPTER 15

"The ghost family house," I said as I looked up at the large exterior.

"The – what?" Theresa asked.

"That is what I call this place," I said. "The Ghost Family House."

Theresa laughed.

"What?"

"That's so stupid," she giggled. "C'mon!" Theresa grabbed my hand and pulled me towards the house. She did as she had done before. She went in through a window from the back of the house and came to the front door to let me inside.

"You seem to know this house really well," I said.

Theresa scoffed at my comment.

"What's up with you?" she asked as we settled down in the living room on the floor.

"What do you mean?" I asked.

"You seem different," she said as she began to take off her clothes.

"Uh -" I laughed nervously. "How so?"

"You're off today," she admitted.

"Yeah, I've been hearing that a lot lately," I said as I thought of Mom-Mom.

"You need something to calm you down?" Theresa

reached into her pants pocket and pulled out a baggie filled with blue pills. She shook the bag at me and smiled.

"No, thanks," I said.

Theresa reached into the bag and pulled out two of the little blue pills. She popped them into her mouth, threw her head back and swallowed.

"I don't get you," Theresa said as she removed her pants. She was now down to just her t-shirt.

"I just don't like taking medicine. I take enough as it is. I mean, I have diabetes. I take insulin for it. I get sick of taking medicine everyday just to function." I could have said more, but didn't want to ruin the moment.

Theresa grinned at me. "Do you take your crazy pills too?"

"I'm not crazy," I said with a stern voice.

Theresa threw up her hands and laughed. "I'm kidding! Calm down, Danny Boy, I'm just fucking with you. Why are your clothes still on?"

I laughed and jumped on top of her. She let out an excited squeal and grabbed a hold of me. She wrapped her arms and legs around me as I caressed her. She kissed me gently at first. Then as she began to get hold of my hair, she began pulling my hair and her kisses turned into bites. She bit my bottom lip hard.

"Ouch!" I exclaimed.

"Come on, take it off," Theresa said as she pulled at my clothes and thrust her body against me from underneath.

As much as I wanted to take my time with her, she made it impossible. Suddenly, my clothes were taken off. She was thriving in my arms and I was trembling inside of her.

Afterward, Theresa decided to smoke my last cigarette from the carton that I stole from my mom. She sat on the floor cross-legged, fully dressed again and puffing away. She didn't even offer me any as she dragged on.

"Why don't you put your clothes back on?" Theresa asked.

I hadn't realized that I was still naked. I didn't care. I had found the drawing pad that I had first drew the living room of the ghost family's house on. The pencil that Theresa had found for me was still inside of it. I was lost in thought, trying to decide what to draw.

"I don't need clothes," I said. "I need to draw."

"You have paper and a pencil," she said as she smoked the rest of the cigarette. "What is holding you back?"

"I can't figure out what to draw," I confessed.

Theresa flipped her colorful hair and pouted her lips at me seductively. "Draw me!" She said with a cute, whiny voice.

I laughed and shook my head.

"Why not?" She pressed on.

"I don't want to see..." I stopped myself. How could I explain it to her?

"You don't want to see...what?" Theresa asked.

"Well," I said as I nervously tapped the pencil to the sketchpad, "how do you see me?"

"What do you mean?"

"I mean, when you look at me. What do you see?"

Theresa laughed.

"I'm serious."

She took a deep puff and let out a heavy sigh, releasing the smoke from her cigarette. Then she said, "A

Gladiator."

"Huh?" I was not expecting that answer. "What does that mean?"

"Never mind!" Theresa said as she gave me a gentle shove. "Draw me!"

I sat the pencil and the sketchpad down on the floor and pushed it away from me. I scooted close to her as she pressed the butt of the cigarette to her tongue to diffuse it.

"Am I not sexy enough for you to draw, but only sexy enough for you to -"

"No!" I shouted.

I seemed to have caught her off guard. She threw the cigarette butt at me and it hit me in the eye.

"Theresa!"

She laughed and began to punch me playfully. "Draw me! Draw me, Danny!" She kept on punching me and laughing hysterically.

Her punches didn't hurt as much as they did in middle school.

"No! Come on. Stop it, Theresa," I said as I grabbed her arms. I squeezed her wrists and she stopped.

"Ice cream," I said.

Theresa laughed harder and tried to break free of my grip. "You want ice cream?" She asked as she struggled.

I wouldn't let her go. She struggled harder, but her laughter kept her from winning.

"No. I want to take you to a concert," I said, hoping that it'll change the subject of me drawing her.

"What does a concert have to do with ice cream?"

"Well, since you're my girlfriend..."

"Only for the week," she clarified.

I remembered the deal I had made with her at Ryan's party. Ignoring it, I continued, "I want to take you on a date."

"Oh yeah? And what are we going to do on this date?"

"There's a concert this weekend for The Ice Cream Man. Come with me."

"Who is the Ice Cream Man?" she asked. She calmed down, but I still held onto her wrists.

"He's a musician. A rapper. He is...uuhh."

"Where did you hear about The Ice Cream Man? That sounds weird."

"He had an impromptu performance and record release party that I had gone to."

"Well, I never heard of him. Where was his record release party?"

"It was...uhh...the other day...ya know, when I was on the train."

"You were on the train?"

"Yeah."

"The public transportation train? As in MARTA Transit?"

"Yeah..."

"At a record release party for The Ice Cream Man?"

"Yeah."

Theresa's facial expression was indescribable. I released her from my grip and both of us burst into laughter.

156

CHAPTER 16

It was nice to see Tom's car in his own driveway and even nicer to walk through the front door and not see him inside of my house. Mom's car wasn't in the driveway either. I figured that she wasn't home from work yet.

Mom-Mom sat in the recliner. She was passed out in front of the television. I watched her chest rise and fall with each calm breath that she took. She looked so frail and thin in her peaceful state of rest. Mom-Mom had graceful features that made her look soft and delicate. I wanted to put a blanket over her and tuck her in the way that she used to do for me when I was a baby. Watching her, I felt my heart begin to break. It scared me to think of myself as a baby. It was even more terrifying to see Mom-Mom age into an old, fragile woman who was asleep in my living room.

"When did you get here?" I heard Mom-Mom say as she opened her eyes.

"I just walked in, Mom-Mom," I said as I plopped down onto the sofa.

"Where have you been?" she asked.

"I was at school," I lied.

Mom-Mom shook her head and said, "Your school called here earlier."

"And?"

"You were not at school," she revealed.

I put my head into my hands and grunted in disbelief.

"Does Mom know?" I asked, afraid.

"No, she doesn't know yet," Mom-Mom said.

I looked over at her, pleading with my eyes. My eyes begged her not to tell on me.

"Mom-Mom," I whined.

"Don't worry," she said as she leaned over and put her tiny hand on my shoulder. "I won't tell her if you promise me something."

"Anything, Mom-Mom," I said.

"Promise me that you will not skip school again."

"Okay, I promise!"

"And!" she said.

"And?" I asked.

"You will come to church with me this weekend," she declared.

"Church?"

"Yes," Mom-Mom said as she raised her chin. "If you don't want me to tell your momma about you skipping school and the school calling here, you have to promise me that you will come to church with me."

I scratched my head.

"I don't know, Mom-Mom."

"Well, I guess I will have to tell your momma when she gets back home from work."

Mom-Mom threw her hands into the air and began to get up from the recliner.

"No! Okay," I gave in. "I will go to church with you this weekend. Please don't tell my mom. And I won't skip school anymore."

"You promise?" she asked.

"Yes! I promise!" I was beginning to get frustrated.

"Good," Mom-Mom sighed with satisfaction.

Mom-Mom got up from the recliner and walked to the kitchen. While she walked away, I felt a sense of panic. Was she really not going to tell on me?

Shortly after, my mom arrived home from work. She looked exhausted. Mom walked into the house and into the living room. She threw herself down onto the sofa and sat down beside me.

"What are you watching?" Mom asked as she stared at the television.

A commercial was on. I shrugged.

"Whatever Mom-Mom is watching," I said.

"Oh Lord, that could be anything with that woman," my mom laughed aloud.

Mom-Mom walked back into the living room with her insulin and a syringe.

"Liz," Mom-Mom began.

I felt my heart almost jump out of my chest.

"What is it, mom?" Mom asked.

"Your son has something he should tell you." Mom-Mom said.

I couldn't believe it! Was she betraying me?

Mom looked at me and waited for an answer.

"What?" Mom said.

My throat felt like it was going to close up on me and I was going to choke to death.

"He is going to church with me this weekend," Mom-Mom revealed.

My mom's eyes widened as if she had never heard of church before. She chuckled and said, "Since when?"

"Since today," Mom-Mom told her. "Daniel said

that he is ready to receive God's Holy Spirit and be cleansed of the sins that ail him."

Mom laughed at me. She shook her head and slapped her knee. Suddenly, her Irish accent seemed to come out of nowhere. It seemed to flare up whenever she was highly amused or incredibly annoyed. I couldn't tell which one was which as she spoke.

"You should get a show. Just don't come back a baptized arse without inviting me to your christening first," Mom said as she let out giggles.

I did not find any of this humorous. I was being taken hostage by my own grandmother! Mom-Mom sat down on the recliner and began to take an insulin shot. My mom got up from the couch and continued laughing as she disappeared down the hall to her bedroom. I looked at Mom-Mom. My head began to hurt. She looked up at me as she pulled the needle from her arm. She smiled and put the syringe into a plastic bag.

"Mom-Mom," I said.

Mom-Mom smiled at me. She said, "Oh, it's okay child. Maybe you going to church will encourage your momma to get her life together and receive the calling of our Lord. God knows, she needs it."

"Isn't that a bit judgmental?" I asked.

Mom-Mom put up her index finger and shook it at me. She answered, "'what business is it of mine to judge those outside the church? Are you not to judge those inside? God will judge those outside.' First Corinthians 5: 12-13."

I was taken aback and silenced. What was I supposed to say to that? At that moment, the house phone rang. It was so loud that it startled both Mom-Mom and me.

My mom shouted from the back, "Will someone answer that?"

I went to reach for the phone on the side table beside the recliner, but Mom-Mom picked it up first.

"Hello," she answered.

There was a silence. For a moment, Mom-Mom looked confused. However, in just a few seconds, her energy felt more calm and mellow. A smiled appeared on her face.

"Who is it?" Mom asked as she entered into the living room. She had changed into her comfortable flannel pajamas.

Mom-Mom looked up and her smile grew bigger. She said into the telephone, "Yes, darling."

I looked at my mom in confusion. Mom shrugged her shoulders.

"Who is it?" she asked again.

"Okay, that is fine, honey," Mom-Mom continued. "Oh, of course we will! She is right here. Hang on a minute and I'll put her on the phone. Yes, uh-huh! That would be wonderful!"

Mom-Mom seemed excited. Eagerly, I began to wonder who was on the other end of the telephone. Mom-Mom told whoever it was on the other end that she loved them. Then she said to whomever it was to hold on. Then she reached the receiver of the telephone out to my mom and nodded to her.

"Who is it?" Mom now whispered.

Mom-Mom shouted in excitement, "It's Manny! Take the telephone, child."

My mom gasped and put her hand over her chest. I froze in shock. I heard my mom let out a deep sigh.

She whispered to Mom-Mom, "What does he

want?"

"He wants to talk to you. He is getting out on early release next week. It was approved! Talk to him!"

Mom-Mom looked at me in excitement. My mom grabbed the phone and began talking to my father, Manny Blackwell.

"Your daddy is coming home," Mom-Mom said to me. She was smiling from ear to ear. "Praise the Lord!" she exclaimed.

I didn't have time to process what was happening until I ran and reached the bathroom. There, I threw up into the toilet and retched out everything that I had inside of me until I was dry heaving only air and my throat burned.

CHAPTER 17

I couldn't sleep that night. I spent most of the night tossing and turning. The garage and that futon were not welcoming for sleep. Summer was near and the heat and humidity that came with it was already sneaking into spring.

I lay awake and stared at the scar on my arm from the dog bite. I tried not to think about that day. I tried to avoid any memory of it. If I thought about it, I could only allow my mind to stop myself from remembering all that had happened on that day. From the moment that I tried to pet the dog, to when I was in the living room having my first bi-polar episode and my father didn't come home that night. The in between was a blur. At least, I *tried* to blur it out of my mind.

I turned on my mobile phone. I had three text messages from E.J. He had asked where I had disappeared to in the first text. In the second text, there was a sex joke that was aimed towards Theresa and me. The last text was about Ryan. In the third text message, E.J. warned me not to cross paths with Ryan because he had heard that Ryan wanted to fight me. I laughed at the last text message. I began to text E.J. back, but my phone suddenly rang. I didn't recognize the number, but I answered anyway, in case it was Theresa. Unfortunately, it was not.

"Did you talk to McKayla?" Christian asked from the other end.

I had forgotten that I had given him my phone number. At that point, I had not yet talked to McKayla.

"Yeah, sure," I said as I pulled at my hair in frustration.

"So, what did she say?" Christian sounded desperate.

"She said meet her at the concert," I pulled out of my ass.

"Wait...what concert?"

"There is a concert going on at..." I pulled the flyer for the Ice Cream Man from my hoodie pocket and continued, "Battery Park on this weekend."

There was a dubious silence on Christian's end of the phone. I hoped he wasn't suspicious. I couldn't say anything. I had to lie to get him off my back for the moment.

"Sweet!" Christian suddenly exclaimed.

"Okay," I sighed in relief.

"Who is playing?" Christian asked.

I slapped myself in the forehead.

"You know what?" Christian chimed in before I could try to come up with a good cover up. "It doesn't matter. I'll be there as long as she's there."

I felt like I was going to lose my mind. I could only think of one thing to ask, "What's Theresa McElheney's phone number?"

Christian gladly gave me Theresa's phone number. I should've had it by now. However, I found myself completely out of thought and right mind when I was around Theresa. Nothing that makes sense ever occurred to me when I was around her. She was like the good kind of any drug that I could have ever been prescribed by a quack like Dr. Eren.

As soon as I hung up with Christian, I called Theresa. She answered the phone. I was surprised that she knew who was calling when she picked up.

"Danny!" she said with excitement in her tone.

"How did you know it was me?" I asked.

She giggled and said, "I have your number."

"How?"

"I have my ways," she teased.

I smiled at the thought of her asking about me to someone who may have already had my phone number, the same as I did to get her phone number. I blushed and forgot why I called.

"What's up?" Theresa asked.

"Oh!" Suddenly, I remembered. "The Ice Cream Man concert."

"What's going on Danny? Are you backing out on our date?"

I was taken aback by her question. She sounded insecure.

"No!" I exclaimed. "I wanted to see if you think McKayla Flemming may want to come to the show."

The line was silent.

"Hello?" I called out.

"Yeah," Theresa sighed. "Why McKayla?"

"Uhhh," I tried to find words for a good lie. "She has good shit."

Theresa began to laugh. "That's all?" she asked.

"Yes," I said, hoping she would believe me. "She can hook us up at the show." One day, I will regret this, I thought to myself.

"You're so right!" Theresa said.

"So, you'll invite McKayla?"

"Yeah," she assured me. "If that's what you want."

I felt a bit of relief. I didn't know what I was going to do besides make sure that Christian would be at the show and that Theresa would make sure that McKayla would be there too. I only wanted it to be Theresa and me, but I found myself in a sticky situation.

"So, I'll see you soon," I said to Theresa.

She responded, "I guess. Are you okay? You sound off."

Before I could answer, my phone began to buzz. I looked down at the caller I.D. and saw that E.J. was calling me. I didn't want to answer and have to talk to him. I'd end up telling him everything that I was already lying about to people. E.J. had that effect on me. He was a good listener. He was too good!

I didn't want to end up panicking and in a pool of tears from frustration and anger. Therefore, I did not pick up the phone. I let it go to voice mail after the normal six rings.

"Danny! Everything okay?" Theresa pressed on.

I realized I had not spoken since she had last asked me if I was okay.

"Yeah," I said. "I'll see you."

"Well...ummm...okay. I guess..." Theresa sounded disappointed. Was she looking for me to say anything else?

Before the urge to tell Theresa that I loved her got the best of me, I pressed the end call button on my phone. I sat up on the futon and stared down at my phone. Should I have hung up on her like that? That was what was so frustrating about being inside of my own head. I felt as if I didn't know how to turn my brain off. I sat up most of the night thinking, no, *over-thinking* about everything. From my love for Theresa to my confusion about Mom-Mom, going to church and seeing my father again.

Almost seven years had passed since I last saw my father. He had been sentenced to 10 years in prison with seven to serve, and the possibility of parole. He was convicted of Aggravated Assault and Battery in the second degree.

The last time I had seen my father was when we were walking in the park together and I tried to pet the German Shepard. My mind wanted me to think about that day, but I tried to push it from my mind. The memory started to blur again.

My mom didn't bring me to the prison to see my father by his own request. He had told my mom that he didn't want me to visit him behind bars. He felt like prison wasn't a good place for children to see their parents.

I know that my father felt badly for being convicted. He seemed ashamed about being in prison because he didn't want me to see him in that place. However, I wondered if he felt sorry about what he had done to be put behind bars. Also, I wondered if my father was sorry for the man in the park who had the dog. More importantly, I was curious if he felt sorry for what he had done to me.

CHAPTER 18

The next day, I did not wake up in time to catch my school bus. I had been up for most of the night due to lack of sleep because my mind was racing with thoughts of *everything*. My mother was not happy about me sleeping in. I woke up to her pinching my arm. She got a good chunk of my skin between her index finger and her thumb and she squeezed the skin so hard that the pain that shot through me was almost excruciating. Nonetheless, I woke up quickly and shouted. I sat up and rubbed my arm. There was a purple bruise beginning to form on my arm where she had injured me.

"What do you think you are doing?" Mom asked me with her hands on her hips. She was hovering over me like a haunting ghost.

"Ouch! Mom!" I cried.

My cries seemed to irritate her. She began slapping me on my shoulders and she tried to hit my face, but I blocked her with my arms. I put my arms up to protect my face. When she couldn't get my face, she slapped the back of my head and my arms.

"I'm sorry! Mom! Stop it! Please!" I screamed.

Mom stopped hitting me and hissed at me. I was afraid to unblock my face. I peeked out at her from between my arms. Her face looked hard and she seemed to be infuriated. I lowered my arms slowly and flinched away from her, just in case she decided to rage out at me again.

"Who do you think you are messing with, kid?" she shouted at me.

I scooted back on the futon to get away from her as best as I could while she hovered and cornered me. She leaned in closer to me and slapped me on my cheek. She got me good! I rubbed my face and felt a single tear jerk from my eye.

"Answer me!" she shouted.

That's when I could smell her breath. She had been drinking. Mom hadn't drank since I was diagnosed with Diabetes. She gave it up because she wanted to improve our diets together. It was a part of our promise to do things as a team and work together to have a healthier lifestyle. That included no sugary foods for me and no alcohol for her.

She broke her promise. It was nine o'clock in the morning and she was already drunk, hitting me and screaming in my face.

"I'm sorry," I said, with more tears flowing from my eyes.

My feelings were hurt more than my face. I think she may have realized what she was doing to me. Mom backed away from me.

"What are you crying for?"

I took a deep breath and wiped my eyes. I said, "You're drunk."

She gasped, seemingly shocked that I had noticed.

"You broke your promise," I said in anger. "You said that you wouldn't drink."

"I broke my promise?" she asked with disdain in her voice. "*You* broke *your* promise, Daniel. *You* were the one to have another one of your episodes. *You* were the one who stayed out all night and worried me. *You* were the one who ate all of my damn cake and had me scared when I couldn't wake you up. *You* made me have to call Tom. And Tom had to give you a shot of insulin to make sure that you were still alive. *You* did this, Daniel! Not me! *You did this!*"

Upset, I hung my head low and grabbed my hair in a rage. I pulled my hair and let myself cry aloud, angrily. I hated when I cried. It gave me terrible headaches. When I cried, the sounds that came from my chest sounded almost inhuman. I felt tears, spit and mucus drench from my face.

Mom didn't care. She didn't back down. She said, "You did this to me, Daniel. We were supposed to be a team. Now, you're late for school. I'm late for work. And I guess you expect me to drive you to school again today."

I shook my head.

"No, you're going!" Mom forced. "Get your ass up and get dressed. You're going to school whether you feel like it or not. I will drop you off before I go into work. Look at you! Making me late for work! Hurry up!"

I stood up and walked towards the door to enter the house from the garage.

"Okay," I said between my angry sobs.

"Get your ass together! When Manny gets home, he won't stand for your shit, Daniel. You had better get it together. Things are about to change around here."

CHAPTER 19

I stood in front of my school, contemplating. Should I go in? Or should I just say screw it? As I was about to walk away, E.J. saw me and shouted my name. I didn't see him until I turned back towards the school. E.J. ran down the stairs and approached me.

He said, "Hey Dan! What's up?"

I shrugged.

"Are you late?"

I shrugged my shoulders while taking a deep breath.

"Okay," E.J. said. "It's almost time for art class. We should get going."

I shrugged. This time I could tell that my apathy annoyed him.

"It's time to present our pieces for the State Art Competition. You have to be there, or you might get disqualified."

Again, I shrugged.

"Are you okay?" He seemed genuinely concerned. However, at the time, I did not see nor care for his kindness.

"What does it matter?" I asked.

E.J. seemed confused. He said, "It matters a lot.

You have so much riding on this, Dan. Don't you want to show these people that you are better than what they think of you? You have a chance to get off academic probation and a chance at an art scholarship. You can't afford to blow it."

"And how can I blow it?" I asked.

E.J. took a deep breath and put his right hand on my right shoulder. He gave it a gentle squeeze and I flinched away from him. He seemed to notice. And he backed off me.

"How can you blow it?" he asked, taking a step back. "You're acting like you don't know. In fact, you are acting like you don't even care!"

"Whatever," I said as I began to walk away from him.

I didn't expect E.J. to come after me, but he did. I began to walk away from the school and E.J. caught up to me.

"Will you tell me what is going on?" E.J. pleaded.

I stopped walking and turned to him. I let the rage that had built up inside of me swell to my head. I felt the temples of my brain throb in anger. A red filter began to film over my eyes.

"*YOU!*" I shouted.

E.J. didn't step back away from me. "Me? What are you talking about?"

"It's *you*, E.J.! It's *your* fault! *You* and Ryan!" I replied with a growl. "*You* talked to Ryan about me and *you* didn't tell me about it. You, him, Theresa and everyone else know about everything! But you're supposed to be my friend. You're supposed to talk to me before you talk to anyone else. If Ryan talks to you about me, don't you think that you should tell me about it?"

"I tried to talk to you!" E.J. yelled.

"No, you didn't!"

"Yes, I did! You wouldn't listen to me. I even tried to call you last night, but your phone was turned off. So, I texted you and you didn't answer me!"

I put my hands to my hair and ran it through to try to sooth myself. If I were angrier, I would have found myself in a fist fight with my best friend. I didn't want that to happen. Therefore, I tried to walk away. But E.J. put his hand on my shoulder again.

"Seriously?" E.J. said. It sounded like there was pain in his voice.

"I don't care," I said as I shrugged his hand off of my shoulder.

He reached out again and grabbed my arm. He said, "Danny, you don't -"

"E!" I shouted at him. At once, he let go of me and took several steps back away from me.

"No," I growled. "I don't care. So, leave me the fuck alone."

E.J. shook his head, turned away from me slowly and walked back towards the school. He seemed hurt as he walked away. I was familiar with that look of pain. I felt the same way when my mom had blamed me for everything that morning. Even though I cared, I felt very little remorse.

CHAPTER 20

It wasn't E.J.'s fault. It wasn't my mother's fault. It was not Mom-Mom's, Tom's nor my Pop's fault. It was all on me. I was ready to stand up to the consequences that I had to face. However, no one said anything when I arrived home.

I had my cell phone on me, but no one had called. That kind of worried me. The worry did not discourage me from going home. I wanted to call Theresa, but I was still upset from earlier.

Following the argument with E.J., I went home. When I walked through the front door, I slipped past Mom-Mom as she slept on the recliner in the living room. I went to my old room, or I should say, Mom-Mom's room. Then I crashed onto her bed. I lay on my back and looked around the room. It was completely different from when I had lived there. I could see that Tom had changed the walls. He had put some weird kind of floral wallpaper on the walls. They had changed my sheets to a solid white color and the comforter was a blue and green paisley design. Very old lady like.

I snuggled under the covers and cuddled with Mom-Mom's four pillows and a blanket. Then I let myself drift off into a peaceful sleep.

CHAPTER 21

I woke up covered in more blankets than what I had over me before I fell asleep. Mom-Mom stood over me smiling down at me and tucking. When I opened my eyes, I freaked out at the sight of her. I had forgotten where I was for a moment and I didn't expect Mom-Mom to be hovered over me. I wiped my eyes and tried to push the blankets off of me, but Mom-Mom kept on trying to tuck me into bed.

"Mom-Mom," I said. "It's too hot."

"You looked cold," she said.

I sat up slowly on the bed and pulled the covers off of me. Mom-Mom sat down on the bed next to me.

"You sleep okay?" Mom-Mom asked.

"Yes, it was nice. You're not mad at me?"

"No, honey. You can sleep in here anytime you want to. Do you like what your momma and Tom did to the room?"

"Sure," I lied.

"I like it too."

I looked at Mom-Mom as she smiled and looked around the room admiringly. She looked so beautiful with her brown skin and long gray hair. Her smile was warm and kind. Without thinking, I hugged her. Mom-Mom wrapped her arms around me and gave me a big, strong squeeze. She was a tiny woman, but she sure was strong. I loved that hug.

"What was that for?" Mom-Mom asked as we pulled away from our embrace.

"I don't know," I said with a shrug. "Maybe for not yelling at me or hitting me for sleeping in your bed."

"That doesn't seem like a reasonable thing to do," she laughed.

I thought back to that morning when my mom had raged out at me. "Maybe you should tell *Elizabeth* that," I said in resentment towards my mother.

Mom-Mom continued to laugh. She seemed to be in a good mood. "So," she calmly said, "Why aren't you in school? Are you skipping again today?"

She spoke softly and without anger in her tone. It kind of worried me.

"Yes," I said. I couldn't lie about it. I had already broken my promise to her.

"What's wrong, baby? You're not feeling well?"

I nodded.

It was true. I was not feeling well. I didn't feel well emotionally. I felt like if I were around people at school, especially if I ran into Ryan or Rex King, I'd negatively lose myself in my emotions. That kind of madness would definitely get me kicked out of school. And Mr. Wolff's office was the last place that I wanted to be. His office always smelled like caramel coffee and peppermint. It was as if he was an old man who was trapped inside of a twenty something year old's body. His face confused me. And he asked me way too many questions that I feel like he should be answering for me. After all, he is the *guidance counselor*. It was better for me to skip school and get my head together.

"What's wrong?" Mom-Mom asked.

I struggled with how I could answer her so that she could understand. I wanted to tell her that I was depressed and angry. I wanted to explain to her how my mood swings were getting the best of me lately. I was afraid that she wouldn't understand.

"My sugar was high," I lied.

"Oh, poor baby!" Mom-Mom exclaimed as she gave me another hug.

"No," I said. "It's okay Mom-Mom. I took my insulin. I will be okay."

She began to make a fuss about making sure that I keep up with testing my blood sugar and eating the right foods. She complained about how my mother didn't feed me well. Mom-Mom expressed her disapproval of how mom kept sweets like cake and sodas around the house, making it hard for me not to be tempted to eat it.

All of the fuss was unnecessary. I knew how to control myself with food, unless my sugar got extremely low. Also, I was good about testing my sugar and taking my insulin regularly. It was the anti-this and anti-thats for my emotional and mental problems that gave me trouble. I'd much rather be able to talk to Mom-Mom, E.J. and even Theresa about those things, but it was too hard. How could they ever understand?

CHAPTER 22

The next day, I got out of going to school because Mom-Mom told my mother that I was having high blood sugars. She didn't tell my mother that I had skipped school the day before. I played the sick card by going along with Mom-Mom's concern for me. Thankfully, my mom hated watching me test my blood sugar and prick myself with needles. Therefore, she didn't ask me to prove how sick I was feeling by watching me test my blood sugar and take my insulin.

The only downside to it was that my mom insisted that I take Mom-Mom to her doctor's appointment since she had to work overtime that day. I drove mom to work and dropped her off. Then I went back home and slept for a little while longer, in Mom-Mom's room. It was okay because Mom-Mom seemed to like the recliner better than her own bed.

When I woke up, Mom-Mom was getting dressed in her room. I was a bit disturbed to see Mom-Mom in her under clothes. But it wasn't as bad as when my mom used to walk around the house naked when I was younger. I'll never be able to unsee these things.

I put a pillow over my face and pretended to be asleep until I could hear that she had left the room. I peeked out from under the pillow when I heard the bedroom door close. She was gone. I was safe to uncover my eyes and stop playing possum. I got out of bed and went into the living room. Mom-Mom was putting on her shoes as I walked in. She looked up at me and smiled. I felt my lips curl up into a smile. Her smile was infectious.

"I'm ready to go," she said.

"Okay," I said.

I grabbed the keys and we made our way to the doctor's office. When we arrived, Mom-Mom checked in and we waited. When the nurse finally called Mom-Mom back to see the doctor, it felt like hours had passed. She got up and I started to get up with her, but she stopped me.

"No, baby," she said. "I'll go in on my own."

"Oh," I said as I sat back down. "Sure. I'll wait right here for you."

Mom-Mom went to the back with a nurse. I felt a sense of worry, but I shook it off quickly. To kill time, I flipped through an out-dated *Time Magazine* that focused on the war in Afghanistan. There were some disturbingly vivid images in that magazine of war heroes and the names and photos of the casualties. I put that magazine down and exchanged it for an older Christmas issue of *O Magazine*. Oprah Winfrey graced the cover. She was dressed in a long, elegant red dress as she stood next to a gaudily decorated Christmas tree and a very young and buff man who was dressed up as Santa Claus. It was an imposter pretending to be Santa Claus, minus the white hair and the beard. He looked like a well fit, tanned and gym sculpted man who was playing dress up in Santa's clothes.

Oprah's smile was warm and bright. Her sparkling

eyes stared widely at a big gift box that was wrapped in gold. The box had a giant, red and velvet bow on top. The young and very manly looking Saint Nicholas held the gift box out to Oprah as she gleamed with excitement. Damn, she's awesome, I thought to myself. I bet she gets really cool gifts from Santa.

Before I could finish reading an interesting article about Oprah's favorite things for Christmas, Mom-Mom came out of the back office. She did not look well. I put the magazine down and rushed to her side.

"Mom-Mom," I said as I opened the exit door for her, "Are you okay?"

"Yes, I'm alright, child. I'm just an old woman," she said as we walked to the car.

When we arrived home, Mom-Mom went to her bedroom and shut the door. It seemed like she didn't want to be bothered, but I knocked on her door anyway. Mom-Mom gave me permission to enter. Mom-Mom lay in her bed on top of the sheets and under her blanket.

"Mom-Mom?"

"Yes, my love?" Mom-Mom answered.

"Can I borrow some money?" I was nervous about asking, but I had to because I was completely broke.

"Hand me my purse," Mom-Mom said without hesitation.

I gave Mom-Mom her purse that lay on top of the dresser. Mom-Mom reached into her purse, grabbed her wallet and pulled out a wad of cash. Without counting the money, she gave me the whole bundle.

"Do you want me to-"

"Child, just take it," Mom-Mom demanded.

"Ummm," I said as I noticed President Benjamin on a few of the bills. "Thanks, Mom-Mom!"

"You're welcome," Mom-Mom said as she lay back down on the bed and closed her eyes.

"Do you want anything?" I asked as I tucked the money away into my hoodie.

"Will you get me a glass of water?"

"Yes, Mom-Mom."

I left the room and went to the kitchen. I poured her a glass of water from the glass water pitcher that we kept in the refrigerator. When I returned to Mom-Mom to give her the water, she was already asleep. I sat the glass of water down next to the nightstand beside the bed. I hovered over her like she had done to me earlier. I smiled down at her as quietly slept. She never snored.

I began to tuck her into the bed. I placed the blanket over her and tucked in the sides.

"Snug as a bug," my Mom-Mom used to say to me when she tucked me in when I was a little kid.

I left Mom-Mom to sleep in peace. I closed her bedroom door and went into the living room. I sat down on the couch and picked up my cell phone. I turned it on to check to see if I had any messages. There were no messages from E.J. I hung my head low and propped my feet up on the couch. I picked at my shoelaces as I began to regret how I had behaved the day before and how I yelled at E.J.

There were a few text messages from Theresa. She wanted to confirm our date for tomorrow night. Also, she assured me that McKayla was going to come to the concert. Theresa made sure to emphasize that McKayla was coming solely to sell me her good stuff. She gave me the prices and the options. Then ended the string of messages with a question. She texted: *Where were you today? McKayla wasn't at school today either. I asked*

FELICIA JOHNSON

your friend E.J. where you were, but he acted weird and didn't tell me anything. What's going on?

Her text message came off sounding a bit insecure, but that wasn't like Theresa, so I didn't continue to harbor on the thought. I texted her back to confirm that we were still going to the concert. I thanked her for inviting McKayla. I threw in there that Christian was coming along, too. Perhaps that would get her to let go of any wild ideas she may have been starting to think about McKayla and me. I pressed send.

Almost immediately, she texted me back: *Where were you today?*

I texted back: *I had to take my grandmother to the doctor.*

She didn't text back after that. I hoped that she believed me. I turned my phone off and put it on the charger since the battery was low.

Mom arrived home. She looked tired. She had a few bags in her hand. I helped her carry them to the kitchen. As we began to put the groceries away, I saw that she had bought a six pack of beer. She put the beer in the fridge. Then she looked at me as I stared at her in silent disappointment.

"Don't look at me like that, Daniel," she said.

"Like what? How am I looking at you?" I asked.

"You're looking at me like you are about to have another one of your fits," she said as she continued to put food away into the refrigerator.

"No," I assured her. "I just wonder why you have beer."

"Your father's coming home next week and you know he loves his favorite beer. He's spent the last seven years in prison. I think that the man deserves a break.

Don't you?"

I wanted to tell her no. Instead, I said nothing. The last time I saw my father he was drunk and then he was being hauled off to jail because of what the alcohol did to him. It made him turn into a monster.

"Did you get the cigarettes?" I asked.

Mom reached into a paper bag and pulled out a pack of Marlboro's. I snatched them from her, eagerly.

"*You're welcome,*" mom said with a tone in her voice.

"*Thank you,*" I replied, mocking her.

She ignored my smart ass reply and asked, "How was grandma's doctor's appointment?"

"I guess it was okay. She seemed quiet and really tired when we got home. She's asleep in the bedroom."

"Thank goodness!" Mom said as she put the last of the groceries away in the pantry. "She has been sleeping on that recliner almost every night in front of the television after all of that hard work Tom put into making the room cozy for her. It's about time she slept in it. How are you doing? You feeling any better today?"

"A little," I lied.

"Thank you anyway, Daniel. I appreciate you taking your grandmother to the doctors today despite you not feeling very well. I just couldn't do it. I had to work overtime to make up for those missing hours yesterday. My boss would have been on my ass if I hadn't stayed late today."

She walked up to me and gave me a light hug with a pat on my back. I stood there without moving as she embraced me. I did not return the hug. She didn't seem to notice or care.

"Are you hungry?" Mom asked as she pulled away

from me.

"Sure," I answered.

"I'll make you, me and Mom-Mom some chicken and mash potatoes with gravy. How does that sound?"

"Sounds good."

"We can all have dinner together for once."

"It'll just be you, me and Mom-Mom, right?" I wanted to be sure that Tom wasn't going to be there. Otherwise, I would kindly pass on the family dinner sit down.

Mom looked at me peculiarly. She tilted her head to the side and put her hands on her wide hips.

"Yes," she said. "Why do you ask?"

"I was just wondering. No big deal."

"Okay, Danny," she said as she pulled out two pots from the utensil cabinet. "Go on and get washed up. Dinner will be done by the time you get out of the shower and you take your insulin."

I did as I was told. I looked forward to dinner with my mom and my grandma. However, when I returned to the kitchen after cleaning up and taking my insulin, I found myself very disappointed. Not only was mom drinking a beer as she set the table for dinner, but Tom was sitting at the table across from Mom-Mom. They were laughing and talking loudly. I stood in the doorway with my arms crossed over my chest. Tom looked up at my mom as she served him with mashed potatoes. She asked if he wanted some gravy.

He said, "Of course! I can't have your delicious mashed potatoes without your famous gravy."

My mother giggled as she said, "I don't know about it being *famous*."

"You know, that gravy is my recipe? It's not hers. I

came up with it and taught her after her and Manny were married," Mom-Mom tattled.

I began to turn away and walk out of the kitchen. They were making me sick. My mom called out to me. I couldn't get away fast enough. I stopped and turned back around.

"Are you coming to eat dinner? I made your favorite with the chicken and mash. I made your buttery, steamed broccoli!" Mom looked so happy.

"Thanks, Mom," I said as I forced myself to sit down at the table. I sat next to Mom-Mom so that my mother would be forced to sit next to Tom. Tom sat across from Mom-Mom. Well, at least I could sit the furthest away from him, I thought to myself.

Mom served me with grilled chicken, mashed potatoes with lots of gravy and, my favorite, broccoli. Everything smelled so good! I ripped into the plate of food as soon as mom gave me a fork.

"Slow down!" Mom said with a laugh. "I swear that boy is trying to choke himself to death."

"It's good, Mom," I said with a mouth full of broccoli.

Mom sucked her teeth and said, "Thank you, but please slow down."

"Let the boy enjoy his food, Liz. He's still growing. That's how boys eat." Mom-Mom laughed.

"So how was the doctor's today?" My mom asked grandma.

"It was fine," Mom-Mom said. She waved her hand as if to shoo something away. "Doctor Marshall wants me to come back next week to run a few tests to see what's going on. He said that from what he could see, he couldn't figure out what's causing all of this pain. So, I go back next Wednesday so that they can poke and prod at me."

"That's certainly what they like to do!" Tom chimed in with a dumb chuckle. "It feels like every time I take a trip to the doctor's, they always want to take my blood."

Mom found him amusing. She laughed as she said, "Same here! Do you think that they could be really vampires? They certainly do take enough blood from you, don't they? You think they're hoarding it?"

Tom replied with a smile. He said, "Seriously! I wonder!"

The trio erupted into loud laughter. I felt like I was in a bad episode of the *Twilight Zone*. As I observed them, I thought to myself that this could not really be happening.

Mom shamelessly guzzled her beer. Tom made himself at home, as he sat next to mom, cutting glances at her, trying to be charming and witty for her and Mom-Mom. And he welcomed himself to as many helpings of our food as he wanted until it was all gone. Mom let him gobble down all of the gravy. Mom-Mom ate her food slowly. She seemed a little too entertained by the queer intruder whom she sat across from at the table.

I could hardly eat anymore of my food because their laughter and joy disturbed me. I forced myself to eat so that my blood sugar wouldn't drop low. As they laughed and joked together, I remained silent. My mother did notice, but she didn't say anything. She would look at me wide eyed. At one point, she kicked me in my shin when I didn't laugh at a stupid joke Tom had made.

I finished eating my food and got up from the table to put my dishes away. Everyone seemed to stop talking all at once as soon as I stood up.

"You going to bed, honey?" Mom-Mom asked.

"Yes, I'm tired. I have school tomorrow." I said as I rinsed off my plate and placed it into the dishwasher.

Mom-Mom nodded and winked at me. I finished putting all of my dishes into the dishwasher and walked back over to the table. Mom-Mom reached her arms out to me for a hug. I hugged her and leaned into to give her a kiss on her cheek.

"You're so sweet," Mom-Mom said as I pulled away from her.

My mother looked bewildered. She didn't say anything, though.

"Have a good night," Mom-Mom told me.

"Good night, Mom-Mom," I said as I started to walk out of the kitchen.

Mom and Tom said goodnight to me in sync with each other. I didn't say anything back to them as I walked out of the kitchen.

I went to the garage and fell onto the futon. I convinced myself that I did well at dinner. As much as I wanted to scream, I kept it together. I did that without taking my anti-this and anti-thats. I began to wonder if I actually needed them anymore. Maybe, I thought to myself, I could see what it's like to be normal.

Still, I had to take my insulin. Otherwise, I could die. My sugar could get too high or too low and I could go into ketoacidosis. I knew that much. But not taking my anti-depressants and the other pills wouldn't necessarily kill me, right? I mean, it's not like not taking my insulin. I decided to let it go and not think about it. I'd just do it. I felt that I could keep it together. I felt like, for once, I could be *normal*.

CHAPTER 23

I sat in homeroom counting down the hours to when school would be over. I was excited about going to the concert with Theresa that night. It was too bad that Christian and McKayla would be there with us.

Mr. Blankenship began role call. On this day, Rex King and his crew of clones didn't bother me. They didn't even look at me. Perhaps the other day when I spoke up did something to make them shut the hell up and leave me alone. Even after homeroom, I saw Ryan in the hallway and he didn't even look at me. I remembered the text message from E.J. where he warned me that Ryan said that he wanted to fight me.

During lunch, I stood outside to smoke. Ryan and a few of his friends walked passed me. Ryan did not shoot one glance at me, let alone express his desire for confrontation. Theresa was there when we passed each other outside. Ryan tried to get her attention, but she walked passed him without saying a word. She came up to me, took the cigarette from my mouth and as I was blowing out smoke, she kissed me!

My eyes were open in surprise. I could see Ryan staring at us and looking just as shocked as I was. Theresa put her arms around me and pulled me closer to her as if our lips pressing together weren't satisfying enough. Right before I closed my eyes, I saw Ryan storm away with his friends who also seemed to be shocked. They murmured and whispered amongst themselves as they walked away.

Finally, Theresa pulled away from me. Her lipstick was smeared all over her face and her colorful hair looked wild and wavy as it blew in the light breeze. She began to laugh. She pointed at me and continued to laugh as I wondered what the hell just happened.

"Can I have my cigarette back?" I asked, confused.

Theresa continued laughing. Then she began to smoke my cigarette.

I sighed. "Okay," I said, "What is going on?"

Theresa reached into her tiny purse that she wore around her shoulder and pulled out a compact. She opened it and handed it to me. I looked into the mirror of the compact and saw Theresa's bright red lipstick smeared all over my lips and partly on my cheek. I took the sleeve of my hoodie and began to wipe the lipstick away.

"No! No! Leave it!" Theresa demanded as she finished my cigarette.

I was annoyed and kept on wiping the lipstick away.

"It looks good on you," Theresa laughed.

When I was sure that all of the lipstick was gone, I closed the compact and gave it back to Theresa. I did not find anything to be funny, but Theresa kept rambling on in her amusement.

"That's a *beautiful* color for you!"

"What are you doing?" I asked her.

"Why so serious?" Theresa asked in a gruff, deep

voice.

"What was that?" I asked, laughing.

"The Joker!"

"No," I said with a smirk.

She was hilarious. It was a poor impression, but it was too cute to ignore. "Damn, Danny! You turn off and on like a light switch," Theresa observed.

"What do you mean?"

"I mean just a second ago you looked like you wanted to fight someone. Now, you're laughing your ass off."

"So, what?" I laughed.

"So, nothing."

I reached into my pocket and pulled out the pack of cigarettes mom had bought for me. I sparked up a new cigarette. Theresa looked like she was contemplating doing something. Just in case, I pulled another cigarette from the pack and held it out to her. She smiled and gladly accepted. She put the cigarette between her lips and I used my lighter to light it for her. Theresa took a deep puff and blew the smoke right in my face.

"You ready for some Ice Cream?" Theresa asked me.

I grinned. She gave me a wide smile. I could feel that she was just as excited as I was about our date. I leaned in and kissed her again. From the corner of my eye, I saw E.J. walking by us. I didn't pull away from Theresa. E.J. looked at us as we kissed and he shook his head. Then he disappeared into the arts building of the school. I guess that I should have felt some kind of remorse or something for the way I had treated E.J. Especially, that day when he walked by and saw Theresa and I kissing, but it didn't occur to me to feel anything.

CHAPTER 24

Theresa and I agreed that she and McKayla would pick me up that night for our date. McKayla was driving. When she pulled up to the house, I was amazed at what I saw. Her car was enviable. She drove a black, convertible Ford Mustang. I smiled, excited as I watched her park her car in my driveway.

Theresa got out, as McKayla waited in the car, and walked up to my door. I ran from the window, threw my hoodie on and tried to get to the door before she could knock. I wasn't fast enough. Mom had already opened the door and let her inside of the house.

Theresa greeted my mom and Mom-Mom with a polite hello. I could already tell that this was not going to be an easy introduction. Mom-Mom already had a disapproving grimace on her face and my mother was probably remembering their first encounter.

It didn't help that Theresa was wearing the best "fuck me" clothes I had ever seen. She had on a black skirt that was so short, I could see that she was wearing black silk panties when she leaned over slightly. Her matching shirt was barely a top as it hung off her shoulders and came down slightly just at her mid-drift. Her leather boots went all of the way up to her knees and folded down at the top. She reminded me of *Puss In Boots*. A very sexy, *Puss In Boots*, if he was a girl that had wavy colorful hair and was wearing his boots. I found myself chuckling at the thought and very excited.

Theresa saw me and reached out to me. I blushed as I hugged her. The looks on Mom-Mom and my mother's faces were hilarious. Mom-Mom looked like she wanted to get a torch and light Theresa on fire as if she was a witch of Salem. My mother looked confused as if she couldn't understand how such a gorgeous girl would get with her unbalanced son.

"You are?" Mom asked.

"Theresa," she said.

"Theresa...what?" Mom-Mom chimed in.

"Theresa...your son's girlfriend?" Theresa said as she looked at me, frowning. Her eyebrow rose, seemingly confused.

"No, hun," Mom corrected, "What is your full name?"

"Leeloominaï Lekatariba Lamina-Tchaï Ekbat De Sebat." Theresa said it so perfectly that I almost burst into laughter.

"I'm sorry, what?" Mom-Mom asked.

My mother did what she always does when she's upset. She put her hands on her hips, cocked her head to the side, and said, "That's your whole name? Do they call you anything for short?"

Theresa looked straight into my mother's eyes and said, "Leeloo."

"Leeloo?" Mom-Mom yelled. It seemed like she was confused and hard of hearing.

"Yes, Leeloo...Dallas..." Theresa replied.

"So," my mother said, seemingly annoyed, "Your

name is Theresa Leeloo Dallas?" My mother wasn't a complete idiot. She had seen the movie Theresa was mocking. In fact, we had a copy of the movie in our collection.

"Don't do it," I whispered to Theresa.

Theresa let out a giggle. Then she turned to me and clicked her tongue at me.

Then, as if things couldn't any more strange, Tom walked into the room. He had been in the kitchen. He was wearing my mother's apron. It wasn't just any kind of apron, either. The illustration on the front of the apron portrayed a cartoon drawing of a naked woman and *all* of her lady parts.

"What the hell?" I heard myself say.

"Are you Danny's dad?" Theresa asked.

"No!" I answered for him. "My father will be here next week. You can meet him then," I said, as I looked at Theresa surprised.

A pained look came over Tom's face. I smiled. I knew what Theresa was doing. She knew that Tom wasn't my father. I loved that she was willing to tug at Tom and my mother so boldly, the way that I wish I could.

"Okay, that makes sense because you look nothing like him," Theresa said with a serious face.

Mom-Mom gasped in shock. I guess it was Theresa's bluntness, among other things.

"I'm Tom Walker," he made clear as he reached out for a handshake. "And you are?"

Theresa gripped his palm and said with a big smile, "Leeloo Dallas...Multi-pass!"

I snatched Theresa's hand away from Tom before I could see the looks on their faces. I heard my mother yelling at me as we ran to McKayla's car. We laughed and held hands until it was time for us to get into the car. We hurried inside and slammed the car doors. No one came to the door to stop me, but I could hear my mother shouting my name. Theresa and I laughed so hard that tears were coming from her eyes. When I saw her laughing that way, open and free, I felt nothing other than pure joy. She was beautiful in that moment. She was my anti-this and anti-that. I wanted things to be like that, always.

McKayla was confused. She shouted, "What's going on?"

"Just hurry up and go!" Theresa yelled, laughing hysterically.

As McKayla sped away, she let the top of the convertible down. The tan leather interior felt comfortable. And it still had a new car smell. I was highly impressed.

"What's with that guy?" Theresa asked.

"Nevermind that idiot," I said. "Is this your car, McKayla?"

McKayla laughed and didn't answer me. She sped up faster and drove onto the ramp to I-85 South.

"You're going the opposite way," I told her.

"It's okay!" She shouted over the wind. "We have to pick up Christian!"

I was not expecting that. I thought that Christian would meet us at the show.

"Christian told me something about coming to the show with us. Theresa asked me if we could all go to the show as a group.

"Thanks again," Theresa said to McKayla.

"It's no problem," McKayla said. "Do you, you know, have my money, Daniel?"

"What?" I shouted over the wind.

Theresa nudged me and held out a bag of weed. Then she leaned forward and whispered into McKayla's ear. I couldn't hear what she told her, but McKayla smiled and seemed happy.

McKayla said, "Great! It should be a good show!"

Theresa sat back and pushed the weed into the pocket of my hoodie. I didn't stop her. Instead, I shook my head and sighed in disappointment.

McKayla pulled up to Christian's house and laid on her horn. Of course, he lived in the same neighborhood as Ryan and his house was just as immaculate.

He had been waiting outside. As soon as we pulled up, he jumped into the front passenger side, next to McKayla. McKayla seemed annoyed as soon as he got into the car.

"Damn, girl!" Christian exclaimed. "Your ride is nice!"

"Yeah," McKayla said as she punched off the clutch and we went speeding off. "Put your seat belts on."

CHAPTER 25

"Are you ready for The Ice Cream Man!?"

A hype man for the rap artist shouted to the crowd in excitement to get us pumped for the show. An opening act called *The Grand Prize Winners From Last Year* came to the stage and began rapping to electronic, pop rock beats. The girls and Christian started making their way to the bar as the music blasted from the stage. I followed them, holding Theresa's hand.

"What contest did they win last year?" I asked Theresa as we approached the bar.

Theresa laughed.

McKayla answered, "They didn't win anything. It's the name of their band."

I was already annoyed. The show was in a much smaller venue than I had expected. It was a room in the basement of a smoke shop, called *Vape & Roots*. I had to pay for all of us to get in. The fee was $10 a person. It was a good thing Mom-Mom gave me some money the day before. When I actually had a chance to count it, I discovered that she had given me a total of $317 total. That paid for our entrance, the baggie of $80 weed from McKayla and drinks for Theresa and McKayla before the show began. I was kind of irritated with Christian because he didn't bother to offer to pay for McKayla's drink. He bought himself a Heineken and went into his own world. He started dancing to the upbeat music.

The venue was relaxed about carding people. I could tell that this show was only about making money. They did not card Theresa or McKayla when they ordered mixed drinks filled with vodka and some kind of schnapps liquor. The two drinks totaled up to $30. That means both drinks were $15 each. Yeah, I thought, they were all about making money and we were the right kind of bait to draw in to this kind of show. I knew right away that this performance was 100% illegal and exploitative to teens like us. Kids who were looking to have a good time.

McKayla and Theresa didn't seem to mind. Christian offered up an already rolled up joint and they lit it up in the middle of the crowd as we pushed our way towards the stage and through the mass of people. McKayla, Theresa and Christian started smoking and passed the roll around to each other. I was concerned at first, but then I realized that they were not the only ones smoking pot. The whole room smelled like the friendly herbal, *loud* grass.

I began to sooth down a bit. I wasn't sure if it was because of noticing that other people were smoking, or if it was because I was getting a second hand high from all of the smoke around me. Whatever it was, it made every worry and cautious cell in my brain melt into warm, carefree molecules. When The Ice Cream Man finally took the stage, I was in a zone of peace, love and dance. I'm sure that I did not know all of the words to Mr. Cream's songs but I found myself trying to rap along. I moved my feet in a semi-rhythmic motion and threw my

hands into the air when the hype man requested it.
Seriously, I had never been to a concert before, and this
first time was the absolute best!

Theresa laughed at me and grabbed onto me as we
bounced up and down in the crowd. Even McKayla
lightened up. She let Christian lift her up onto his
shoulders. She sat atop on the back of his neck as he held
her up with great body strength. She hollered at the
Atlanta Rapper as he asked where all of the fine ladies
were in the house. Then he dedicated his next song, the
final song, to those lovely women.

When the song started, I got so excited that I
jumped up and down.

"Them girls with the Big Booty In Da Flesh!"
shouted The Ice Cream Man. His hype man started his
affirmations shouting, "YEAH!" and "UH-HUH! and
"OKAY!". The deep beats to the familiar hip-hop song
began to pump from the speakers. I remembered my ride
on the train. It was the song that I liked. This song made
me want to come to his show.

Turning towards Theresa, I said, "I know this song!
This is the one that reminds me of you!"

Theresa smiled and grabbed a hold of me.
Suddenly, everything slowed down. She leaned into me
and wrapped her warm arms completely around me. Both
arms were around my neck. She grabbed a hold of the top
of my hoodie and pulled it back. My wild and messy hair
flowed out. She grabbed a hold of it with both hands and
pulled me close to her.

Suddenly, there was no music. There was no
crowd. There was no McKayla and there was no
Christian. Everything went silent and we were the only
ones there, in the middle of the dance floor and in front

of the stage. I saw, felt and heard only Theresa. Her breaths were heavy and slow.

She leaned into me with her eyes wide open. As I leaned into her, I felt her breath on my face, smelled her sweet sweat and felt her voluptuous softness with my arms touching her hips and my hands around her waist. I loved it. She responded to my touch by pulling me closer so that our foreheads pressed together. Her expression was calm, confident and a little bit of something I was not familiar with yet. She kept her eyes open and focused on me.

Before I kissed her, I closed my eyes and said, "Theresa, I love you."

CHAPTER 26

After the show, the high did not seem to wear off immediately. It was a non-stop smoke fest in the basement of *Vape & Roots*. Oh, I get it now, I thought to myself as we walked out into the night, after the show.

Theresa held onto my arm and walked alongside of me. She wasn't smiling or laughing like she had been before the show ended. She was silent and seemed stoic.

"Are you okay?" I asked.

Without saying a word, she nodded.

"Did you have fun?"

She nodded again.

"What's up?"

She stopped walking and said, "I'm just tired."

At that moment, a loud sound of thunder crackled in the sky. Little droplets of rain began falling down. I put my hand out and caught some of the stinging raindrops.

"Where are McKayla and Christian?" I asked.

Theresa shrugged. We looked around the crowd for them, but they were nowhere to be found. I turned on my cell phone and tried to dial Christian on his phone, but it went straight to voice mail.

"I can't get him," I told Theresa.

"Let's go to where they parked the car," she suggested.

She grabbed my hand and led the way as we tried to run from the increasingly falling raindrops. When we reached the parking lot, most of the cars were already gone, including McKayla's.

"Are you serous?" Theresa screamed.

That's when the loudest sound of thunder came from the sky. The crackling sound was so strong that it sounded like it broke the earth. Instead of buildings falling down and balls of fire falling from the sky, we saw a bright light hail from the sky and create a great show of lightening.

"No!" Theresa screamed in anger.

"It's okay!" I said. "Let's try to get to the train station."

The rain was really coming down now. We were getting soaked. The lightening and thunder did not make it any better. I could see the fear and frustration on Theresa's face. Her demeanor quickly went from calm to afraid. She held onto me tightly as we tried to huddle under an awning in front of a building near the parking lot.

"It's too far!" Theresa cried.

"It's not that bad of a walk," I assured her. "Come on! I know my way around."

I took her hand and we ran out into the storm. The rain fell so hard that we could hardly see where we were going. At some point, I had to stop and look at the street signs. I thought that I knew where I was going, but I felt lost.

"Why are we stopping?" Theresa asked.

"Um...I thought that the train station was this way,

but I -"

Suddenly, a bolt of lightening hit a rod on top of a church near where we were standing. It lit up the sky and made a crackling noise. It scared Theresa so badly that she grabbed onto me and buried her face into my hoodie. She shivered and shook so hard that it felt like she was having a seizure. I had to get her out of the storm.

"Screw it!" I said.

I picked Theresa up and carried her in my arms. Theresa held on to me tightly. Her arms were wrapped around my neck and her face stayed planted between my neck and my shoulder. Emory Hospital was just across the way. I carried her all of the way there.

When we were safely out of the storm and sheltered near the hospital's entrance, I put Theresa down and let her stand on up on her own. Theresa looked around.

"Come on," I said to her while offering her my hand.

"What are you doing?" Theresa asked with a frightened look on her face.

"We can wait out the storm in here. It's okay. It's just a hospital."

I began to walk to the entrance. Theresa didn't take my hand, but she started following me. The automatic doors opened and I stepped inside, but Theresa stopped short just before entering. The automatic doors remained open as I stood inside and Theresa stood at the threshold.

"What's wrong?" I asked her.

Theresa shook her head in a swift and panicking motion. She wrung her hands and her wrists. Then she started pacing back and forth from the threshold and back towards the storm. This caused the automatic doors to open and shut continuously until I stepped outside.

"No! No! No!" Theresa panicked.

When she came back towards the doors, I stood just outside and grabbed a hold of her. I wrapped my arms around her and hugged her.

"Okay," I said. "We can just stand outside here in the front. We don't have to go inside."

"No, please," she said, smothering her face into my hoodie. Her voice sounded muffled, as she cried, "Not here. Please."

"Theresa, there is nowhere else to go," I told her. "I don't know any other place around here, open this late that will let us stay there to wait out the storm."

"I can't," she pleaded. "Please, no, I can't."

She began to shiver again. This time was more violent. I had to look at her to make sure she was still with me. She looked up at me. Her teeth chattered and her eyes were red with tears. I couldn't tell if she was crying or if it was because of the rain. However, the way that she looked at me, pleading with her eyes and making herself vulnerable to me by clinging to me, trustingly, I couldn't deny her request to get away from the hospital.

"I don't know what you want me to do," I said, defeated.

Theresa continued to hold onto me. She looked around from side to side. Then she sighed deeply as if she had figured something out, but didn't want to say what it was that she was thinking.

Hesitating, she said, "I-I...um," she tried to say through chattering teeth, "I may know a place."

"Where?" I asked.

"Come on," Theresa demanded. She grabbed my hand and we ran back into the storm.

Theresa didn't seem as afraid of the storm as she had been before. Perhaps because she seemed to know where she was and where she was going. I ran behind her, following her stride. She kicked her feet up and took long leaps. I was surprised that she could run that fast in her boots.

We ran for about six blocks and through four intersections. We reached a neighborhood that had a stone wall border and a gate to get inside of the complex. Theresa pulled a white card from her tiny purse and swiped it at the gate. The gate slowly opened and we walked inside. The inside of the neighborhood was lined with rows of townhouses, two car garages and backyards with swimming pools. It was too dark and rainy to get a good look at everything, but it looked very different from my neighborhood and Ryan's place.

We came upon a house that was made of bricks. Theresa led me through the two-car garage that she opened from a side door that she had opened with a key. We went through another door that she opened with another key and we entered into a narrow hallway. The hallway was white, plain and had hardwood floors. Theresa locked the door behind us and led me down the hallway. We were drenched! Rainwater dripped from our clothes as we walked, creating a trail of droplets. If I get lost in here, I thought to myself, I could at least find my way out by following the trail we left behind. I chuckled at the thought. Then Theresa shushed me. I quickly shut my mouth.

At the end of the hallway, we entered into a kitchen. The kitchen also had hardwood floors and the walls were painted white. It had hardwood cabinets and stainless steel appliances. Everything looked shiny and spotless. Not a dish in the sink or a used napkin on the floor. There was a set of chef knives next to a cookie jar. The cookie jar had a cartoon of a fat chef holding a plate of freshly baked cookies. I stopped and opened the cookie jar. I took a delicious looking oatmeal raisin cookie out and tried to put the lid back on. Instead of it actually snapping into place, it fell from my grip, hit the side of the counter and crashed to the floor. The lid shattered to pieces upon hitting the floor. The noise from the lid breaking scared Theresa. She turned around, noticing that I had strayed away from her, and she quickly grabbed my hand and pulled me into a laundry room.

"Sorry!" I shouted, sort of panicking with her.

Theresa shushed me again and we stood still inside of the tiny laundry room.

"*I'm sorry,*" I thought I had whispered.

However, Theresa put her hand over my mouth and took the cookie from me. I frowned. She leaned against me as I stood against the wall. The space was very confining, but I felt like it was exactly where we needed to be. We stood like that for a few minutes until Theresa felt it was safe to stick her head out of the door to see if anyone was out there. With her hand still over my mouth, she tucked her head back inside and closed the door. Then she removed her hand from my mouth and gave me back the cookie. I ripped into it.

Theresa began taking off her clothes and ringing them out into a small sink that stood under a shelf, next to the washing machine. The shelf had all kinds of cleansers, bleach, detergents and fabric softeners. They were the fancy kind of products that you saw on television commercials that had bears and other cuddly animals that could talk to sell the brand.

"What are you doing?" Theresa asked. "Take your clothes off and ring them out."

I finished off my cookie and did as I was told. I took my clothes off and immediately began to shiver. It was freezing in there. When we were naked, Theresa put our clothes into the washing machine and poured in some of the fancy snuggle bear kind of detergent. Then she started the wash.

"Please God, I hope Kat slacked off today," Theresa said as she opened the dryer. "Yes!" She exclaimed in a whisper as she began to pull laundry from the dryer. "The one day that I can actually count on Kat to not be so perfect cleaning this place, I lucked out."

Theresa tossed me a towel and pink terry cloth robe. I looked at her dubiously.

"What? Dry off and put that on. There is a pair of slippers there, too. Put those on."

"Really?" I said, holding up the pink robe and looking down at the matching slippers.

"Put it on," Theresa laughed. "It's okay. It's one of my robes and I'm sure you can fit the slippers. I kind of have big feet. Anyways, you can take them off when you get to my room. I can't have you scuttling through my house barefoot and naked."

It didn't occur to me that we were actually at Theresa's house. It hit me the moment that I put on her robe, felt its softness, and smelled the fresh, powerful smell of expensive fabric softener that I knew this was Theresa's home and she actually let me come inside of her home. There was not much time to enjoy my realization. Theresa put on her slippers, wrapped a towel around her body and put on a red, silk robe. Then we rushed out of the laundry room. I felt as if we were being sneaky. Someone could catch us and we needed to be careful. We were in a hurry again.

"Should I clean that up?" I asked, pointing to the broken cookie jar lid on the kitchen floor.

"No!" Theresa half whispered. "We have to get to my room."

"Theresa!" A woman's voice shouted from upstairs.

"Oh shit!" Theresa said. We hurried through the cozy looking living room. There was a fireplace and a fur rug in front of it. The living room was large. It was decorated with family photos upon the fireplace and on the walls. It had a chocolate leather sofa, love seat and a cool looking recliner set up in a neat way in front of an amazing, 70", HD smart television.

"Wow!" I said.

"Theresa? Honey? Is that you? Are you home?" The woman asked again. She sounded like she was walking towards the stairs from a dark hallway upstairs.

Quickly, we reached a door downstairs that was next to a half bathroom. Theresa pushed me into the dark room and shut the door. She stood on the other side of the door and I could hear her talking to someone. I didn't turn on the light for fear that, whomever she was talking to might discover me. With the way Theresa was acting, I knew that would not be good for her and probably not for me either. So, I stayed quiet, waiting in the dark room.

After Theresa and the woman stopped talking, Theresa opened the door and stepped inside.

"Don't forget, dear!" I heard the woman shout from the top of the stairs.

"Good night, Mom," Theresa said as she closed the door.

Theresa turned on a floor lamp that was made of red wood and linen shades. It looked like a large Japanese lantern lamp. It dimly lit the room and gave it a warm glow. I looked around the purple painted room. Little golden stars stuck to the walls with a moon and astrology sign decals. I touched the wall decals. They looked so real. Theresa watched me as I wandered her room. A cherry wood framed mirror sat atop her matching dresser. Two photos were on the mirror. One photo was a picture of a young man. He had light brown hair and big blue eyes. His smile reminded me of Theresa's, infectious and bright. The other photo was of this young man and girl that looked like a younger version of Theresa, minus the make up and the girl's hair was blonde. The two smiled in the photo. The photo was a close zoomed in shot of their faces. They looked alike.

"Who is that?" I asked pointing to the photo of the two people.

"That is my brother," Theresa said.

"And is that you in the photo with him?"

Theresa came up and stood beside me. She took the photo down from the mirror and stared at it. She nodded and then held the photo out to me. Not sure why she wanted me to hold it, kindly, I took it from her and gave her a little smile. I looked down at it.

"It was our first time at Disney World," Theresa began. "Neither of us had been. But when mom got married to Dennis, we were finally able to go. Instead of taking a honeymoon with just the two of them, they decided to bring us along with them. It was like a family honeymoon kind of thing." Theresa paused, looked down at the photo as I held it. She laughed. "Have you ever heard of such a thing?"

"No," I chuckled. Then I handed the photo back to her. Something about the photo gave me a strange vibe. I felt like I knew something, but as I searched my mind I couldn't find it right away.

"You and your brother look alike," I said with a smile, hoping she'd tell me more.

Theresa held onto the photo and sat down on her bed. She stared at it silently and laughed to herself. Perhaps she was recalling a funny moment they had on their vacation, family honeymoon.

I continued to look around. There were lots of books about the stars and planets. Apparently, she was into astrology and science. Her floor was covered in a deep purple, fringe carpet. It was comfortable and spotless, much like the other parts of the house.

Looking through her books, one caught my attention. It appeared to be a poetry book. I picked up the frayed and aged book. Theresa immediately rushed to my side. She took the book out of my hands.

"Wait," I said. "I want to see that."

"What for?" Theresa said as she held the book and the photo of her brother to her chest, protectively.

"It looks interesting," I said, laughing. "Come on, Theresa. You're being silly."

Theresa seemed to think about it for a moment. Perhaps she did realize that she was being silly over a book. She laughed at herself and handed the book over to me. I looked at her as I took it from her, smiling and still sort of laughing at her behavior.

When she settled back down on the bed, I took off her robe and hung it up on one of her bedposts to her bed. Her queen size bed was also made of cherry wood. It had a large backboard and strong frame and four tall posts at each corner.

I sat down on her bed beside her, still wrapped in the towel she had given me and I settled in next to her. The mattress and her purple, fluffy comforter were super soft. Much better than the futon I slept on. Theresa leaned her head on my shoulder and sighed.

The front cover of the book was worn, much like the rest of it, but I could make out the title. The book was called, *Abysmal Vein: A Collection of Poetry From The Greats*.

"Abysmal Vein? Who is that?" I asked.

"I assume that it is a pseudonym of some great philosopher and literary genius," Theresa said with a shrug. "This book has a great collection of poems by famous and infamous poets from throughout the centuries. I believe the oldest one dates back to Socrates."

Impressed, I opened the obviously antique book very gently as to not let it fall apart. It had a weak spine, but the pages still held together. On the first page, the printing revealed that it was a first edition and it had been published in 1912. I gasped.

"This book is older than my grandmother," I laughed aloud.

Theresa chuckled. She said, "That's funny. My brother said the same thing when he gave it to me right before he went to baseball camp. The last time I saw him." Her voice softly trailed off on the last thing that she had said.

I continued to flip through the pages. I saw a few poems from the dark and intriguing Edgar Allan Poe, a snippet of a sonnet from Shakespeare's King Lear, two frightening pieces from *The Lamentations of Mary* and *The Divine Comedy* and a poem from Socrates' time, just as Theresa had said. It was a poem by Plato called *To Stella*.

I stopped on that page and read the poem by the former student of the great Socrates:

> *"Thou gazest on the stars, my star!*
> *Ah! would that I might be*
> *Myself those skies with myriad eyes,*
> *That I might gaze on thee."*

"Yeah, Plato was smooth," Theresa said. "I'm sure Stella dropped her panties for him as soon as it was published."

"Haha! Probably," I laughed.

Theresa took the book from me and turned to a page that had a golden silk cord pressed into the crease, creating an elegant bookmark for the page.

"This is what I want to show you," Theresa said. She pointed to a poem called *Spartacus*. A poet named Leigh Gordon Giltner wrote it. "Read it," Theresa encouraged.

Aloud, I read:

> *He stands storm-browed, imperial, chief*
> *Of all Rome's gladiators; brave*
> *Beyond all others; fearless in belief,*
> *A captive--but no slave.*
> *His brow is like a god's--a brow of power,*
> *Lips soft with human sweetness--ere the day*
> *He entered the arena, and the hour*
> *He first beheld man's life-blood mixed with clay.*
> *Felt rise within him bestial strange desires*
> *And savage instincts in a brutal heart*
> *That battened on men's blood; burned with unhallowed*
> *fires*

Of slaughter--till--a thing apart,
A hired butcher of his fellow men, he stands
Daring the fasting lion in his den,
Or some fierce gladiator on the blood-stained sands,--
A savage chief of yet more savage men!
He stands, with massive throat and thews of steel,
While loud acclaims the listening heavens fill,
And Roman women smile. He does not know; or feel
A moment's joy or one triumphant thrill.
He heeds them not. He sees as in a dream
His home and Cyrasella's citron groves;
A youth again, beside some purling stream,
With gladsome heart and joyous pipe he roves.
He sees anon that gentle shepherd boy,
Who knew no harsher sound than plaining flute,
In the arena stand--Rome's sport and toy--
A bestial, bloodstained hireling brute....
Then swift thro' every throbbing, pulsing vein
The fierce unconquered spirit of old Sparta ran.
Rome's fiercest gladiator is to-day again
A Thracian--and a man!

"Whoa!" was all I could manage to say. "That was heavy. Powerful!"

Theresa took the book from me and looked down at the poem. She touched the words with her fingers and ran them across the page.

"It was Damian's favorite," she said. "He said that this poem described, perfectly, what it felt like when he was on the playing field. He'd read it before every game he pitched for. No matter what team he played for, I believe that he gave it his all. No matter what other people said about him. Like a Gladiator. Damian gave me this book before he played his last game."

I remembered! I knew the two faces in Theresa's picture. The photo was of the son and the daughter-mouse from the ghost family house. And the son was a famous baseball player. He played for several teams in the American Major League Baseball. His name was Damian McElheney. Theresa was the daughter-mouse, sister of the famous baseball player!

"Oh my god," I said, realizing and feeling excited, heartbroken and dumb all at once.

"Do you remember when you asked me what I saw when I looked at you?" Theresa asked, with tears in her eyes.

"Yes," I said softly as I placed my hands gently on her cheeks.

"You're a Gladiator, Danny Boy," she said with a heavy sigh.

I didn't really know what she meant. I didn't know how to feel in that moment. It was too much, but I kept my head together and tried to focus on her and listen to what she had to say. Theresa looked up at me with her big beautiful eyes and tears began to fall heavily. Her tears streaked down her face and landed on my hands. It was fine with me. I held on to her and let her rub her face into the palms of my hands so that I could comfort her.

Theresa choked out, "You remind me of him sometimes. You are strong, brave and sometimes you're a beast. Then there are times when you scare me. You've always scared me. Even in middle school when we used to fight. I fought you because I didn't understand you. Now, you're in my home and I see you here. You're so...so..."

"I'm sorry," I said.

Theresa shook her head and pulled away from me. She continued to cry as she read a line from the poem. She read, "*Of all Rome's gladiators; brave. Beyond all others; fearless in belief. A captive--but no slave.*"

Then she looked up at me. "Do you know what that means when I think of you and my brother?"

"No," I admitted. I couldn't even imagine.

"That there is light in you. A part of you is so courageous. You can be fearless and put yourself over other people's B.S., Danny. It's the you that everyone sees when you're out in the world and you are shining brightly when you are doing the things that you do. However, there is a darker side. A side that you try to hide. No one can see it unless they're looking for it or care to know what it is."

She looked back down at the poem and ran her fingers along the page again. I waited for her to continue to tell me what she saw in me. She was going deeper than anyone I had ever known before. Not even E.J. went this deeply into my veins.

Theresa continued reading. This time, it was from near the ending part of the poem. She read, "*He sees anon that gentle shepherd boy, Who knew no harsher sound than plaining flute. In the arena stand--Rome's sport and toy--A bestial, blood-stained hireling brute.*"

When she finished reading, she closed the book and sat it back on the shelf. I was speechless. Everything was hitting me all at once. I felt sad, heartbroken for her, excited, curious and somewhat defeated.

"The drugs killed him," Theresa cried over by the bookshelf.

I wanted to get up and hold her, but I wasn't sure if I should touch her. We both were in a state of mixed emotions. She was obviously still grieving the loss of her brother. He died from an overdose on prescription pills while on the road with the New York Yankees as they headed off to play the San Francisco Giants.

Damian McElheney was a fierce and mighty pitcher. He had some of the best stats a pitcher could ever get in Major League Baseball. In a whole season, Damian was 25 and 5 with a 2.07 ERA. This man had 105 strikeouts in his last season with the Yankees! He was a superstar! However, no matter how good he was as a player, for some reason, though, he couldn't stick with one team. He was always being traded. The last team he played with was the New York Yankees. His last season was his best.

When he passed away, the word of his death and all of the gruesome details of his drug use were plastered all over the news. Teammates, coaches, lawyers and even some of his family members that were interviewed by the media claimed to have not known about his problem with drugs. However, Theresa knew. She was the quiet daughter-mouse who saw everything and stayed quiet, in her own words.

The guilt and pain killed her inside. Then I realized that was how the daughter-mouse became a monster. She blamed herself.

"I should have told someone when I saw what he was doing," Theresa continued to cry. "When he got injured while playing for the Red Sox, he had to take time off to heal his arm. He was traded while he was going through physical therapy. I think that did something to him. That's when I saw that he was getting stronger, faster and the pain seemed to go away," she snapped her fingers, "like that! It seemed like it was too soon for him to go back to work, but he had to because he knew that if he stayed out too long, he was traded again. So, he just kept taking the pain pills and he drank. I watched him change and slowly kill himself. But I didn't say anything because no one else was saying anything. I heard about his death on the news. Our mom and Dennis didn't even tell me. They let me sit in front of the television and watch strangers tell me when they knew all along!"

Theresa ran over to the bed and threw herself into my arms. I held on to her and squeezed her as she gripped onto me tightly.

"I let him go. I can't let you go, Danny," Theresa said.

"I'm not going anywhere," I promised her.

"Everyone is like a corpse. They go on with life as if nothing matters. I hate it here. Mom throws her parties and people shower her with compliments and pity. She eats it up and she loves it. Dennis was great! He was so good to us after our father passed away and he married my mother. Although, they were having an affair before my father died. My father had spent months in the hospital before he died. We all knew it was coming. He was already at stage four when he was diagnosed. The doctors said that the only thing they could do for our father was to make him comfortable. It's not easy to sit beside someone you love as they take their last breath. They just stare at you with their eyes wide open and lay there helpless. You feel so...so... "

Theresa drifted off into thought and seemed to be replaying the death of her father in her mind. She seemed to be lost for words in describing that moment. Suddenly, she seemed to snap right out of her memory trance.

"Anyway, I think that's when mom started seeing Dennis. Then when Damian died, I think Dennis died too. He is still breathing and walking around, but he buries himself in alcohol and work. I know he loved us as if we were his own children. And now he has allowed himself to become someone whom we don't even know."

"I know how you feel," I admitted.

Theresa looked up at me as I held her. She looked somewhat surprised. She said, "What do you mean?"

"My father drank, too," I said. "And his drinking caused him to do some really dumb things. He was good to me like your dad was good to you and your brother. But when my Pop started drinking, he did bad things that constantly put him in jail. That's where he is now. But he does get out of there next week."

"Do you think he'll start drinking again?" Theresa asked.

I shrugged my shoulders.

"Dennis has been to rehab about six times, but he slips up every time he gets out. It's crazy. They say that alcohol and drug addiction is a mental illness. You know, like those people who have depression or schizophrenia and have to take pills so that they don't jump off a roof or go on a killing spree or something. It doesn't even seem close to anything like that. Do you believe in that stuff?"

I sat frozen, still holding on to her. I wanted to answer her, but I was torn inside. She caused me emotional pain, but I couldn't reveal myself to her like I wanted to. I was so close to opening up to her that night.

"I don't know what it's like to be addicted to alcohol or drugs," I said. "But do you think that people, who take drugs and die from it, like Damian did, mean to kill themselves? Or are they looking to get their fix again and it just goes wrong?"

Theresa sat up and pulled herself away from me again. This time she looked me straight in the eyes. That scary expression appeared on her face again. She gave me the look that I swore to myself I'd never say or do anything to have to see that look again. I messed up.

"My brother didn't commit suicide," she said, sternly.

"No, I wasn't suggesting that. I was just trying to understand why professionals would say that addiction can be considered to be a part of mental illness," I said. I was trying to choose my words carefully. I was already walking a fine line.

"Nothing against people who have so called mental issues, but I don't think they are the same thing. I think that people get sad and angry all of the time just like people can be happy and stupid, kind of like my mother," she said with a slight laugh.

I shrugged my shoulders and lay back on the bed silently. Theresa lay down next to me. We stared up at the ceiling in silence for a few minutes.

"You know what we should do?" Theresa said as she turned her head towards me.

I continued to stare at the ceiling. I still felt defeated and sad. However, I indulged her.

"What should we do?" I asked her.

"We should get the hell out of here," she suggested.

"It's still storming out. We should at least wait for the rain to calm down."

"No, Danny. That's not what I mean," Theresa said as she nudged me.

It felt like she was trying to get me to look at her.

So, I looked at her and she stopped nudging me.

"Then what do you mean?"

"I mean we should, like, run away. Go somewhere far away from these walking corpses. My home is like a morgue. And you hate it here, too, right? I mean, we hardly go to school and they'll probably kick us out anyway. Best we leave before the shit-storm," Theresa said, now smiling.

I rolled onto my side to face her. She rolled over too. I pushed my hands through her soft hair. It was still a little wet.

"Now, that," I said, more cheerfully, "Is an awesome idea."

"Really?" Theresa asked. I could tell that she was serious and growing excited.

I thought about it before I answered her. I tried to picture my life if I decided to stay. I lived in a garage, slept on a crummy futon, hated my meddling neighbor, my father was coming home and I had no idea how life was going to be if he and my mom started drinking again. Theresa was right. I was probably going to get kicked out of school because of my academic probation. It was not going well. My grades sucked because I never did any homework.

Then I pictured my life on the road with Theresa. I'd be with the woman that I loved. I would wake up beside her every single day. We could live together and make love whenever we wanted. We wouldn't have to sneak around. I wouldn't need anything but her and my insulin. And of course, we needed food. The rest of what we do and what happens to us would be our choice. No one could tell us what to do or how to live. Our lives would be our own and we could live our lives to the fullest, together.

"Yeah, really." I said. "Let's do it."

PART TWO
(MONSTER)

PREVIEW

Dr. Finch was the first doctor that I ever had that wanted me to talk about it. Still, I felt uncomfortable as I sat in the chair across from him. I picked at my shoelaces and kept my head down. He was waiting for me to answer him, but I had no idea where to start. It was frustrating, trying to find the right words to explain the how and why I was in the hospital in the first place.

"It's okay," Dr. Finch said. "I'll ask you in another way. Why did you ask to come to Bent Creek? You could have gone home after you were released from Egleston Hospital."

"I guess..." I said with a heavy sigh, "I guess it was because I had no other place to go."

"What do you mean?"

"I mean that I couldn't go back home after everything that had happened. It was hard for them."

"It was hard for whom?"

"Mom-Mom, my Mom and my Pop and Theresa..."

"What about you?"

"What about me?"

"Since you've been here, you have only talked

about everyone else's problems, but what about you?"

"I don't know," I admitted.

Dr. Finch didn't look like he was buying it. He shook his head and gestured his hands out to me as he spoke, as if he was pleading with me.

"Look, Daniel," Dr. Finch said. "I know that it's not easy. Especially when you have been through all that you've gone through in the last week. The emotional stress on top of your physical stress from the complications you suffered with Diabetes, it's-"

I don't know what came over me. I put up my hand to stop Dr. Finch from speaking and I cut him off.

I said, "Having diabetes isn't the real challenge. Sure, I have to stick myself with a needle about 2 times a day. I have complications if I don't watch it and take care of myself. Like, I can't eat what everyone else eats like candy bars and birthday cake. I can live with that. I always have lived with it. It's the Bi-Polar Disorder that messes me up. One minute I'm fine and as soon as something happens that makes me angry, I lose it. It's like when I last saw Theresa talking to Ryan, I just wanted to kill him." I paused and looked out of the window. Still picking at my shoelaces, I tried to calm down. It felt like my emotions wanted to get the best of me. I didn't want to cry. I couldn't cry!

Dr. Finch remained calm and quiet. He watched me and listened to me intently. It was a strange feeling to have someone listen and care the way that Dr. Finch seemed to care about what I had been through before coming to Bent Creek.

I continued, "I don't understand Bi-Polar like I understand diabetes. Diabetes is simple. It's genetic. My grandmother has it and my father has it. Maybe Bi-polar is genetic too? I don't know."

Dr. Finch nodded his head and remained silent. I kind of expected him to tell me if it was true or not. I wondered if it was genetic. I expected him to hit me with some popular statistic or something. I looked at him and something about his concerned expression made me chuckle. He made me a bit anxious. The next few words out of my mouth seemed to spill out without thought.

"When I was a kid, I watched my father beat a man into a coma. I didn't do anything to help the man. I just stood there and watched as my father beat the man's face into a bloody pile of meat with his bare hands. I didn't cry. I didn't scream. I didn't react at all. I even had a bad dog bite from the guy's German Shepard. I still didn't show any emotions. My dad just spent the last few years in jail for it and came home last week. We never talk about it. My mom tried to talk to me about it one time, but I didn't know what to say. Mom concluded that I was in shock and she didn't press me anymore about it."

Dr. Finch's eyebrows rose up. He opened his mouth as if he was about to say something, but I didn't let him. I started to laugh and he shut his mouth. He looked at me questionably.

I continued to laugh as I said, "I guess that I've been in shock for the past seven years."

OK DANNY BOY
By Felicia Johnson

PART TWO
(MONSTER)

COMING SOON!

ABOUT THE AUTHOR

Felicia Johnson is an author, motivational speaker, and mental health and youth advocate. Felicia Johnson began writing when she was six years old. Writing has been her saving grace and she is an avid advocate of journaling. Felicia is an avid reader and encourages aspiring writers to journal at least once a day.

Using her own moving story of her survival from child abuse, homelessness as a teenager, and overcoming self-harm and depression, as well as her education in Psychology, Felicia raises awareness about mental health issues and abuse. She also promotes prevention of suicide and child abuse by advocating for youth and friends and families of survivors. Felicia is a youth mentor for Youth Villages and is a writer and speaker with the Personality Disorder Awareness Network (PDAN).

Felicia was nominated for the Gutsy Gals Inspire Me Award of 2014 and her best-selling novel entitled "HER" was nominated for the Georgia Writer's Association Author of the Year Award. In addition, Felicia was honored and awarded for speaking and organizing the Women's Empowerment Event 2015 for National Alliance On Mental Illness (NAMI) Augusta, GA. As a survivor of child abuse and one who deals with mental illness in her personal and work life, Felicia is very involved in efforts to end the stigma of mental illness.

Felicia Johnson currently lives in Atlanta, GA with her husband and their cat named Eren Jaegar.

Printed in Great Britain
by Amazon